THE LAS VEGAS AFFAIR

Johnny Lebaron arrives in Las Vegas, leaving behind an unhappy marriage in New York. His hopes of a quiet vacation are dashed when he meets the beautiful Dulcie Grande. Only recently out of jail, she seeks vengeance on the man who put her there — crooked casino owner Nat Franz. Johnny and Dulcie, caught up in her vendetta against Franz, must fight for their lives against organised crime and a psychotic hit man with orders to kill them . . .

Books by Norman Lazenby
in the Linford Mystery Library:

I NEVER KILLED
WE THE CONDEMNED
DEATH IN THE STARS
DEAD SINNERS
SWARTHYFACE
PAY BACK
LITA'S LAMENT

NORMAN LAZENBY

THE
LAS VEGAS
AFFAIR

Complete and Unabridged

LINFORD
Leicester

First published in Great Britain

First Linford Edition
published 2010

British Library CIP Data

Lazenby, Norman A. (Norman Austin)
The Las Vegas affair. - -
(Linford mystery library)
1. Women ex-convicts- -Fiction. 2. Organized
crime- -Fiction. 3. Murder for hire- -Fiction.
4. Las Vegas (Nev.)- -Fiction. 5. Suspense
fiction. 6. Large type books.
I. Title II. Series
813.5'4–dc22

ISBN 978–1–44480–145–3

Published by
F. A. Thorpe (Publishing)
Anstey, Leicestershire

Set by Words & Graphics Ltd.
Anstey, Leicestershire
Printed and bound in Great Britain by
T. J. International Ltd., Padstow, Cornwall

This book is printed on acid-free paper

1

The sun was a brassy orb and the temperature well over the 100F mark that afternoon when Johnny Lebaron came out of his Las Vegas hotel. He stood on the sidewalk and thought bitterly of the swift changes an airplane trip can make.

He wondered how Doris, his wife, still in New York, was accepting the fact that he had left her, beat it, or whatever you cared to call it! Sure. She'd be humiliated, furious, insulted. She'd have all the words.

He felt no remorse at having walked out on his wife. It wasn't as if he was leaving her destitute. Her rich father would take care of the financial side of things.

Well, he wasn't going back. Three years of being married to Doris and he was sick. It wasn't her fault because in many ways she was a mighty fine gal. So maybe it was his fault. He was restless. He was the guy that wanted to be free. That, of

1

course, was the merry ha-ha, because no man who went looking for freedom ever got it.

Johnny Lebaron saw the girl again. She came out of his hotel and walked past him. Apparently she was staying at the Rainbow Hotel. As she walked away, he stared at her burningly, for a long time.

He'd seen her before, in the hotel lounge. She was strikingly all colour. She wore a white linen suit that fitted almost too snugly. She was the inevitable blonde and he guessed she got it out of a bottle, but what the hell! Her hair was soft, long, silky. Red lips looked like soft cushions against a creamy skin. She wore a defiant expression as if ready to fight at a moment's notice. He wondered why.

There would probably be a girl for him in Las Vegas. He had not left Doris three thousand miles back to stare at Nevada scenery. Sure, thoughts like this made him the complete heel, but that was the way he felt and he couldn't help it. The girl walked into a garage. Johnny followed, slowly. He thought he was behaving like a low punk, but maybe this was okay in the new set-up. He wasn't Doris's engineer hubby any more; the good guy who obeyed and toed the line because nice Doris had a rich father and Papa was the guy behind the monthly paycheck. Nope, he wasn't that guy any more.

The girl with the defiant expression got into a cream convertible and tooled it to the gas pumps.

Johnny Lebaron smiled faintly and walked over to her auto. His quizzical grey eyes met blue, inquiring ones. She was flawless in a close-up. She laughed softly. 'Okay. I've seen you before — in the hotel. Your name's Johnny Lebaron.'

He raised an eyebrow. He did not realise he looked damned attractive to girls. In three years with Doris, he had forgotten.

'How'd you get my name?'

'The hotel register.'

'Oh, sure.' He smiled into her eyes again. 'Usually the other way around. The guy finds the girl's name! I'm alone in this town. How about you?'

She gave a swift, wary glance over her

shoulder; then at the stream of autos on the road. 'I'm like that old Hollywood star — I want to be alone, but not all the time, so get in. I think I need help from a guy like you!'

He muffled an exclamation; but he got in and slammed the door shut. The station attendant finished filling with gas and water. She tooled the convertible out of the driveway and joined the other quick-moving slugs on the road. She went right down Wentworth Boulevard; turned up San Pedro Street.

'All right,' he said. 'Give. There's somethin' queer about it, isn't there? What's your name?'

'Dulcie Grande. Now look, Mister Lebaron — you're big and husky. Maybe you can help me!'

She looked down narrowly at the plain ring he wore. 'You married?'

'Yes.'

'All the best men are married,' she said automatically. 'But not necessarily the best women. I'm not.'

With a swift, feminine movement she zipped open a white handbag that lay on the seat beside her. With another whisk of her hand, she presented him with a squat, heavy gun.

He looked at it with interest and flicked it open.

'You know how to use it?'

'I was in the Army. Who do I kill: the Chief of Police or the peevish ex-boyfriend?'

'Don't be a fool!' she hissed. 'Stick it in your pocket — hold it. And come with me.'

She slipped out of the car and stood on the sidewalk. She was tallish; just the right height, Johnny Lebaron decided. He wondered if she was crazy. He supposed there could be beautiful lunatics.

'This way,' she said, and she walked across the sidewalk and into the courtyard of a casino. Johnny noticed the place was the usual white stucco, flat-roofed and backed by a clump of palms. He read the dead neon: IMPERIAL CASINO.

'Look, baby,' he said. 'You give me a gun and tell me to follow you. What are you tryin' to frame on me? What gives? You look nice — even lovely! Come up with something that makes sense and you got me.'

'Look, I'll explain later.' Blue eyes challenged him. 'There's a guy in this casino. All you got to do is stick right behind me. I'm counting on you. Look tough. You're big enough. I'll talk to the guy. He's a chiseller called Nat Franz — the oily so-and-so!'

Johnny Lebaron shrugged. 'Okay. So what! Go ahead — confront the oily chiseller. I'll be listening. If you're crazy, it's certainly a pity. If you're not, I'll be behind you. What have I got to lose? I came out here for a hell-around anyway!'

'That's what I figured long ago,' she said surprisingly, and she walked on.

The Imperial Casino, like all the licensed gaming houses in Las Vegas, was closed during the afternoon. The business started when the neons sneered at the sun going down, and really warmed up when the man-made glare of green, yellow and red burned against the purple night. Just now the dive looked dead.

They walked up the steps. He admired her from the rear. She wasn't, of course, anything like Doris, except that the two of them were female.

They went through the door, walked along a walnut-panelled corridor. He glanced into a room where some gaming tables stood orderly and clean after the attentions of the chars. Then he took two long strides and came up behind Dulcie. He put his hands lightly on her shoulders as she stopped at a rich-looking door that announced: PRIVATE.

She didn't knock. She turned the handle. The door opened and she walked in. Johnny thought that this was where he had to act wary. Pretty soon he'd know if the girl was mad or not.

Beyond the door was a small lobby and a glass door. Dulcie opened it and Johnny, walking in close behind her, thrust one hand into his gun-pocket.

They were inside an apartment. They stood in a living room where broadloom softened every footstep. There was nice furniture, a settee and a big guy reclining on it. He lowered his morning newspaper abruptly and his feet swung to the carpet. He uttered a rasping sound, just like a cur with a bone.

'You! Get to hell outa here!'

'I want my dough,' snapped Dulcie. 'The dough you promised me three years ago. This is the second time of asking, Nat Franz! I want it! Ten grand! C'mon, you heel! You've got to give me it!'

Nat Franz folded his newspaper and rose to his feet. Johnny, looking at him carefully, saw that the squaring act thrust out the man's belly. This man was no fitter than an over-fed pig.

'Get out, Dulcie, an' take your pal with you. Ten grand! You're crazy! Ain't you heard how expensive it is runnin' a joint like this? I can't put my hands on that kind of lettuce these days.'

She sneered: 'How — you — lie! You owe me ten grand. From three years ago. From the days I worked a racket with you. Ten grand — my share of a cute proposition we tied up. Only I never got the dough. You held onto it, and I went to the pen — for three years, you damned heel!'

'The cops put you in — not me!' he jerked. He had lowered his head and his thick lips were looking ugly. He darted an odd glance at Johnny Lebaron.

'Yeah? Queer how you stayed in the clear and the cops got a tag on me! Well forget it, slob! That was three years ago — in Los Angeles.' She was still spitting like a mountain cat. 'I've had three years of hell. You — huh — you've built up this gambling den and I guess my ten grand helped a lot. I'm not even bothering you for the interest. Just start getting the ten grand.'

Nat Franz walked slowly around the room. Johnny and Dulcie turned as he walked. Nat went to a window and looked out.

'I could call a cop.'

'You and cops!'

'You're demandin' money with menaces. I don't know anythin' about your ten grand. That's on the record if you've brought this lug along as a sorta witness. Who is he, anyway?'

'He's a great guy, and he'll help me. Get a gun on him, Johnny!'

Johnny Lebaron produced the gun and pointed it steadily.

Nat Franz froze. His lips were parted; his eyes stared narrowly at Johnny.

Johnny Lebaron glanced down momentarily at the gun.

He wondered what the devil he had gotten into. All this for a girl! He knew nothing about her except for her last few venomous remarks, and they painted a grim picture.

This was a laugh. He had run away from a possessive wife to meet up with a crazy woman. A Miss Dynamite, no less!

Now the gun was out. It felt like a drainpipe. So he had to go on. But he couldn't trigger. Murder was murder! Even when science had made it so easy so that all a guy had to do was move a finger.

Nat Franz licked enough saliva onto his lips to say: 'Tell him to quit kiddin', Dulcie. You can't shoot me. There are people on these premises — cleaners — people — '

'There isn't anyone!' snapped the girl. 'I figured that out. Now get into your office and open that safe. I bet you've got at least ten grand stacked away there!'

Johnny Lebaron whistled silently, and felt sweat under his hatband.

2

They were inside a small room that seemed a blend of study and office: three silent, tensed people. Nat Franz got within a yard of a big steel safe and hesitated

'This is a mistake, Dulcie. Ya playin' this all wrong. I won't like this.'

'You've got dough in there!' she exclaimed triumphantly. 'Get it out!'

Nat moved sullenly, but the whites of his eyes warned Johnny. The next moment the man was diving for the gun. Hands clawed forcibly, clumsily against Johnny's arms and wrists.

Johnny Lebaron reacted quickly. His instinct was to fight back, but with his fists. He pulled the gun away from clawing fingers, and shoved it into his jacket pocket, then rammed an uppercut to Nat's chin. The blow travelled only a short distance before it connected and jerked the flabby man's head backwards.

Nat went right back against the wall. Suddenly livid, he shot out a hand and grabbed at a paperweight lying on the desk. Johnny stopped the weighted fist in mid-air by closing his hand around it. Another twist of hands and arms and Nat Franz was in the grip of a wrestling lock.

The struggle ceased. Nat knew when things were his way and when they were not. Johnny got a close-up of his eyes and they weren't pleasant.

'You're my man!' breathed Dulcie. 'Now, look, he's got a key for this safe.'

Johnny glanced sideways. 'It's a combination. I guess he's the only one who can open that job.'

'All right. Make him!'

He looked at Nat Franz whose eyes reminded him of a mongrel with the rabies. 'You heard what the lady said. She wants her ten grand so get it out — or I'll open the thing myself. I'm an engineer and locks and autos are my meat.'

That bit was strictly bluff. In case Nat saw through it, he applied more pressure to the wrestling hold. There was nothing else to do. Someone had to lose.

Nat, accustomed to criminals and not knowing anything about the guy who held him, gave in, made a few deft turns of the combination and then brought his hand away. Dulcie moved in and thrust long fingers into the safe.

Some minutes later she had a pile of bills, mostly hundred-spots, and counted out nearly fifteen grand while her eyes glistened.

'They look nice! Maybe I ought to allow myself some interest! What do I get for three years of hell? Say another couple of thousands?'

Johnny said grimly: 'You take ten grand and no more.'

Her sea-blue eyes widened. 'You're honest! What do you know! All right, I'll play along with you, Johnny boy. I'll take my ten grand only.'

She stuffed the wad of bills in her white handbag, then thrust the rest of the papers and money back into the safe.

'Let's go. He won't holler. And he won't phone the cops. That isn't the way he operates.'

They went out into the living room. It

was a backwards form of motion, with Nat following up wearing a vicious expression. Johnny guessed that the guy's brain was racing around a score of vengeful plans.

Nat Franz apparently did not dredge up one that could be applied immediately, for some moments later Johnny and the girl were swiftly crossing the court. They reached the cream auto and jumped in. The girl drove away fast, tooled around a corner and rolled the auto into the parking lot of an inn. The place was hung with neon tubes that said — LITTLE JOE'S. ALES, WINES AND SPIRITS.

Johnny offered her his cigarettes. She glanced at the inscription on the case.

'What was wrong with you and Doris?'

'A lot.'

'Okay. To hell with Doris. You've sure helped me. Let's have a drink right here.'

'Wait.' He turned his head and looked at her intently. She had a shapely little nose. Her lips held a suggestion of a pout. They were too red, but it suited her. He noted the soft, flawless skin and the supple erectness of her shoulders under

14

the linen suit. 'Are you on the level with all this spiel about three years in jail and the ten grand and Nat chiselling you?'

She took the cigarette out of her lips and breathed: 'You fool, of course. Do you think I'm absolutely rotten? Oh, I know I'm reckless, bad! I've paid for it, too. I've done the three years. I don't owe society anything now. Get that, Johnny boy! I'm as good as you. And you're so honest!'

He tightened his lips, and grabbed at her wrist.

'Quit trying to rile me!'

The movement brought her near to him. He looked down at her unsmilingly for a moment, and then he kissed her, almost brutally.

'Don't rile me and don't try to fool me!' he snapped. 'Let's go get that drink. I think I need it.'

Inside the bar it was cool. Some fans and air-conditioners operated smoothly and silently. Three men and two women sat at the cocktail bar. Johnny and Dulcie went to a booth with a martini and an ale. They sat in silence for some minutes watching each other and thinking.

'You're some baby!'

'You're nice.'

She opened her white handbag and brought out a small red-leather notebook. She stared at it for a moment, then Johnny, prompted by a swift hunch, reached out and plucked it from her fingers.

'You took this from the safe!'

'Yeah' — defiantly. 'Give it to me.'

'This book belongs to Nat Franz. Looks pretty important — full of addresses. Wonder what it's all about?'

She leaned forward and smiled bewitchingly. 'Suppose we find out? I figured it was important the moment I saw it.'

'I told you to put the stuff back.'

'Sure, you did. But it's such a nice little notebook, and I thought it looked important.'

He began to read. He got through the first two pages, and then he looked into Dulcie's eyes.

'Nat evidently has sidelines. This is a record of some transactions and the people concerned are finally described as dead, debt cancelled. Sounds darned queer!'

'Let me have a look.' She read with a tiny frown that fascinated Johnny Lebaron. Still watching her, he drank deeply of the iced ale.

'Yeah,' she said. 'It's always the same. Always this dead, debt cancelled note at the end of a number of transactions under a person's name. And he's got five names down here — all men. This is Nat's handwriting, sure enough. I'd know it anywhere. Queer! How come he got that dough from these five guys? And then how come these five guys are listed as dead?'

'Gambling debts?' hazarded Johnny.

'Maybe.' She stared at the book, scanning columns of figures that didn't make sense to her. 'Queer these guys should die after paying up their debts.'

'People are always dying. Maybe Nat keeps tag of all his customers.'

'Casino gambling is mostly cash,' she retorted. 'I don't see why he should keep tag on his customers. They either win or lose. And guys like Nat aren't sucker enough to give credit. Even in Nevada you can't collect on a gambling debt. By golly, this is real queer!'

'I'm a New Yorker and I don't know much about Las Vegas casinos. How about you? I don't know yet where you come from.'

'Los Angeles.' Then she sneered, 'And the pen! But never mind. This notebook interests me.'

'Why?'

'Look, Mister, I can read you like a comic book. I had you figured out in the Rainbow Hotel. Honest Joe! Let's stick together, huh, for the time you're in this town! But don't try telling me what I should do. Don't try to straighten me up. You might as well know I want to get the edge on Nat Franz and make him suffer. Maybe I've got my ten grand, but I got a dirty deal from him, and I can't forget it.'

Johnny finished his ale. 'Gawd, you talk a lot!'

'Just to give you the lowdown, brother.'

He put his hand out and said grimly: 'Give me that notebook. You'll land in more trouble if you start foolin' and nosing into the affairs of guys like Nat Franz.'

Temper suddenly blazed from those sea-blue eyes. 'Nothing doing! You — '

He tried to grab at her hand, but she moved fast, slipping to one side of the booth, still holding the red-leather notebook. He sliced around the table after her, but she darted away like a fish in water and by the time he got out of the booth she was at the door.

When he got to the exit, she was moving swiftly over the parking lot, and reaching her auto she dived in. With lips tightened to a straight line, he broke into a run. Still she beat him to it. The engine whined and then leaped forward only to have his fingers brush the door handle.

Then he was just a guy lumbering after a vehicle. She sliced for the road and surged into the traffic stream with scant regard for safety. He was left behind. Finally, he halted on the sidewalk and watched her auto disappear.

He had her number. 7XL12. And he'd know her car anywhere. He'd know the gal, too! By heaven, he'd know her! He had never quite met anyone like her.

Johnny turned slowly and went back into Little Joe's. He wondered if he would see her again. Because if he didn't do something for her, he was sure she'd blow herself up!

He realised with a sudden laugh that she would have to return to the Rainbow Hotel if only to check out.

He drank the rye; slid off the stool and headed fast for the door. In the street he hailed a cab, jumped in and slammed the door.

'Rainbow Hotel. Pico Avenue.'

Minutes later he was back at the hotel. He went inside and looked through the lounge, then into the bar and out again. The heavy gun in his pocket felt awkward, forcing him to keep one hand bunched over it.

He couldn't see her anywhere, so he walked along the street to the garage. It was there that he saw Dulcie Grande again.

She was sitting in her cream convertible, not in the garage, but at the start of the driveway. There was a man sitting beside her, and Dulcie was staring at him viciously. The man, a thin, lean specimen, was watching her warily. A brand new hat shaded a long lean jaw, and a mouth thinner than a piece of string. He was holding a gun to her ribs.

3

Johnny advanced on the man's blind side. Then Dulcie saw him.

'One of Nat's gunnies!' she breathed. 'He wants me to go back to the Imperial Casino. Tell him where to get off, Johnny!'

Johnny's grey eyes flashed a warning at the hood as he twirled. His leveled gun added to the threat.

'Okay,' muttered the hood. 'Okay. There'll be another time.'

'Get to hell out of that auto,' snapped Johnny.

The man snicked the door open and slid out. He didn't measure up to Johnny Lebaron's height, but he stood near him and exchanged unpleasant sneers.

'Beat it,' said Johnny. 'And don't try anything again with Miss Grande.'

The man sniggered. 'Miss Grande — hell! Look feller, you've got a lot to learn. Nat Franz hires guys like me to knock the smartness outa punks like you.

Okay, so this play didn't come off. I should worry. Next time I see ya, feller, you won't wear that lousy grin. Ya can't front Ed Kibe an' get away with it.'

Johnny swung a balled fist with accuracy and speed. It cracked against Ed Kibe's long jaw like a coconut split by a wooden ball. The man staggered back, shoes grating for a firm footing, then made off unsteadily.

'Give me that damned notebook!' Johnny shoved a hand to the girl.

'Don't start all that again,' she said wearily. 'Look, I want to get checked out of this hotel. Nat knows I'm here. That guy was waiting for me.'

'How did he know you were here?'

'I asked Nat Franz for my dough once before and didn't get it. He must have checked on me then.'

'Give me that notebook and I'll send it to Nat Franz by special messenger.'

'Don't get monotonous, Johnny.' Dulcie climbed out of the auto, displaying an expanse of creamy flesh. 'Now let's get out of here. Nat can be real mean. It isn't that he goes in for tough play himself, but can hire thugs — knows all the angles. He was like that in the old days.'

He saw the sense of her argument. Nat would best him as an opponent. That wasn't so good; and even if the notebook were returned there was still the little matter of ten grand.

'What now?' she asked when they had checked out of the hotel, and were driving down Wentworth Boulevard. 'Nat won't let up.'

'Maybe you should get out of town while you're still safe.'

'I'm not finished with Nat.'

He nodded while she scraped past a crimson bus and stopped for lights. He reached for her white handbag and zipped it open before she could stop him. He took out the red-leather notebook and pushed it into his pocket.

'Okay, pal!' she hissed. 'I'll get it back. Right now, maybe you've got some ideas where we should stop?'

'Hit the highway for Los Angeles. You might be safe in that cement jungle. It's only a four hundred mile trip.'

'Aw, turn it off. I'm staying in Las

Vegas until I find out what's behind the 'dead, debt cancelled' gimmick.'

He took a deep breath. 'All right. One push, baby, and you'll be going down the slippery slope. I'd better stick with you a bit longer.'

'Hell, quit that smug way of talking!' she blazed. 'Have you ever had to fight your way through life? I came right out of the lousiest slum you could ever find in this God's country. I didn't have to look for rackets — I was in them! Guys like Nat Franz — and others I could mention! Then the pen.'

'Yes, I know,' he muttered. 'But — '

'Aw, turn it off! Let's drop it.'

She drove on. One moment she was damnably attractive, and then the next she disgusted him. He thought he ought to spank her. Maybe he would, at that, some time.

Before she realised it, they were driving on the outskirts of Las Vegas. She tooled the auto down the four-lane highway, heading out of town. A white sign said: U.S. 63. They were on the numbered highway.

'Going to L.A.?' he asked. 'If so, head for Baker. It's okay with me. I don't care where I go.'

'Don't be a sap. Quit repeating yourself. I'm staying in Las Vegas.' She seemed to have something in mind, and a bit later drove up to one of the many motels that stood on various sites alongside the highway. She drove down a red gravel driveway to an office and restaurant with neat rows of chalets lying beyond. The parking lot held a number of autos.

'One cabin?' asked the guy in the office.

'Make it two,' Johnny grated. 'We ain't married.'

The man said: 'So what!'

They were handed keys and shown the adjacent chalets.

Dulcie rolled the auto into the parking lot. When she came to her cabin, she threw her bag in and then went to Johnny's door.

'So proper, aren't you?' she sneered. 'Well, you needn't think I'd have had it any other way.'

'Just what are we doing here?' demanded Johnny.

'It's a place to live. We're only two miles out of town. And Nat Franz won't know.'

Johnny felt the weight of the Smith and Wesson again in his pocket. 'Okay. I'm on the loose, anyway. Maybe it would be something else if it wasn't you. Beat it. I'm going to change my shirt.'

She gave him a mocking glance and moved away. He was washing when Dulcie crept back, and didn't see her pull his jacket off the chair. Her lithe fingers dipped into his pocket and extracted the red-leather notebook. Then, as silently as she had arrived, she slid away. Johnny continued to wash vigorously and make gurgling noises.

It was only later, when he went through his coat pockets, that he found the notebook had gone. He had patted his pockets absent-mindedly, more or less, to check on cigarettes and lighter. He was alerted fast enough when he realised the book had vanished. He went around to see Dulcie.

'Look, baby, this game of tag has to stop. Give me the book and I'll mail it right away to Nat. He'll get it tomorrow.'

'You're nuts. I've hidden it, and I don't mean in this cabin. Now don't get all het up. Instead, take me to the restaurant for something to eat. I've changed — look! How do you like it?'

She posed, just like she'd seen models do. She looked terribly attractive in a green dress that curved to her. With her shimmering blonde hair, red lips and childish eyes, she was a living pin-up. She knew it. She smiled impishly at him.

Out of a dry throat, he said: 'You look good! Swell . . . Okay, we'll eat.'

All the same, he walked around her cabin and looked in the lockers and shelves. He even looked into her hand-bag, whipped up cushions, stared into the locker that held the folding bed, but without finding the notebook.

'All right,' he snarled. 'The hell with it! Heaven help the guy who marries you!'

It was some time later, after they had eaten, that Dulcie went into a phone booth, and got through to the Imperial Casino and Nat Franz. 'Hiyah, Nat! It's Dulcie. You still sore? You are? Sure. Well listen, you lug. I'm going to make you pay. Not in cash — I've got my ten grand. I figure you put the cops onto me three years ago. I took the rap. Well, I'm going to put the cops on to you and I've a hunch it'll be the death chamber, pal. How'd you like the idea?'

'You're crazy,' came Nat's voice, thick with anger. 'Stop talkin' like that! This is a public line. Just get this, Dulcie: you're playin' with fire. You an' that hobo you picked up. Give me that notebook back. Mail it, see, or you'll regret this smart play.'

'Brother, you sure make me curious. I'm going to look into that book pretty thoroughly.'

'Mail it an' I'll forget about the ten grand!'

'Ha-ha. You can forget about the ten grand in any case. It's gone to Dulcie Grande. You owed me the dough, remember?'

'You little fool — '

'Nuts!' she said, and cradled the instrument.

She came out of the telephone booth feeling exultant without stopping to think whether the move had been smart or not.

She didn't care to analyse things.

Johnny watched her narrowly. He wondered what sort of crazy action she contemplated.

She went into her cabin and he heard the door click slowly. He walked over and tried the door. She had locked it. He went to the lighted window. He saw her mocking smile, and then she pulled down the blind. He guessed she was studying the little red notebook.

He stood and smoked a cigarette and thought that she was some bitch. What could he do about it?

He could go back to New York that night by plane, just like he had arrived, and leave Dulcie Grande to hell around and come to the grief that surely awaited her.

Only, he wouldn't. Maybe he couldn't. Maybe he was falling crazily in love.

Johnny mooched disconsolately around the motel for the next hour. Returning to the chalet, he noticed the light was still on. He could see a glint of it through the blind. He tested the door but found it still locked.

He cursed her under his breath and walked away aimlessly. His eyes swung over the parking lot, and then he jerked to a halt. The cream convertible had gone. A minute's examination of the lot clinched the fact. So she had locked her door behind her, leaving the light on and the blinds down to trick him! Obviously she was away back to town.

This assumption was perfectly right. Dulcie was speeding along the highway. She entered Las Vegas city limits and turned the auto up into one of the swank residential districts. There was an odour of money around the places like Gilbert Avenue and Pasadena Avenue. The houses stood a long way back from the road, on landscaped lots. Some were Hollywood ideas of Spanish architecture.

Dulcie tooled her auto up the driveway of one big house and halted yards from the main door. She liked the white paint and red roses.

She had gotten the address out of Nat Franz's little notebook. According to Nat, the man who had owned the house was dead.

4

Dulcie Grande had the confidence of a woman with an intoxicating appearance. A Japanese manservant had ushered her into the house. She walked across soft carpet and sat poised on a settee.

The young man who came forward to greet her smiled eagerly from the first moment his eyes blinked at her With a guy smiling so widely as that, Dulcie figured she could extract even the gold from his teeth.

'Are you Martin Greg?' she cooed.

'Oh, no,' he said quickly. 'That was my father. He's dead, I'm afraid.'

She knew that. It said so in Nat's little confidential book.

'Oh!'

'I am Randolph Greg. Can I help you, Miss Grande?'

'Well, it isn't much. I once knew your father. He often came to a nightclub where I worked. I've been out of town for some time. I've just got back and wondered why he didn't seem to be around.'

'Didn't you hear? He was murdered.'

'Murder!' The exclamation was genuine. She had read in Nat's notebook, 'dead, debt cancelled', and had wondered, that was all. If Greg had been murdered, what about the other four listed in the book?

'The police never discovered the culprit,' Randolph said bitterly. 'It happened about four months ago.'

'But it's so awful. Poor Martin! I told you I just got back to town. Do you mind if I ask questions?'

'Not if you really want to know about it.'

'Sure I do. He was a good friend.' Dulcie sounded convincing.

Randolph licked his lips hesitantly. 'He was being blackmailed.'

'Blackmail! That's dreadful. Why, gee, no one is safe! Did the police ever get to know who it was?'

Randolph Greg shook his head. 'No. The swine was covered up nicely. I guess only Dad knew him.'

Dulcie crossed her legs with a smooth, calculated movement. Randolph followed the movement with hungry eyes. 'He was shot in his own grounds. The police believe a silenced gun was used. Certainly no one heard the shot. The killer got away in his own time apparently. So terribly simple!'

'Of course, the blackmailer killed your father?'

'The police guessed so. The trouble was Dad left no papers that might point to the fact that he was being blackmailed. After the murder, I realised he'd been secretive about a number of telephone calls he'd had, but at the time I never gave them a thought. Dad had many activities that he never explained to me — why should he? I told the police about the phone calls afterwards but there wasn't the slightest lead arising out of that. No one knew why he was being blackmailed until after his death, when the sums of money he had withdrawn were revealed. He gave this swine some fifty thousand dollars in three separate payments!'

Dulcie gasped, thinking of Nat Franz. A bubble of choking excitement rose inside her. She had no doubts that Nat Franz was the blackmailer, and probably the murderer, too, although maybe he had hired a gunny to do the killing.

She gathered her breath for another question. 'I wonder — I really wonder why Martin was blackmailed? Did you ever learn what sort of hold this guy had on him?'

'No. There wasn't a letter or a note. All that seems to have happened, if you want it in its basics, is that Dad paid out fifty grand to this unknown guy, probably on threats which we know nothing of, and then met his death by a silenced gun. No more than that.'

Randolph Greg rose grimly and walked to the window, probably to conceal his feelings. Dulcie realised she had questioned long enough. She knew plenty now. Boy, the things she knew!

'I'm so dreadfully sorry!' she murmured, moving over to him. Her nearness seemed to effect a rapid change in his emotions. He smiled again.

'Don't let's talk about it. We can do nothing. It's just something on a police dossier, and I guess with the present crime wave they'll forget it. About you, Miss Grande' — and here his voice became deeply interested — 'did you say you were working in a nightclub? I shall have to go along and see you.'

Dulcie never wavered. 'Oh, I'm not working at the moment. Right now I'm having a little rest. But when I get my next job I'll give you a ring and let you know.'

She was still smiling teasingly when she left the mock Spanish house and climbed into her auto. Randolph saw her off. As her car disappeared down the driveway, he realised he was a poor sort of guy. He hadn't even got her telephone number.

Dulcie drove away and halted the car in another street. She had so much to muse over, she could not be bothered to drive. And in any case, she wanted to study again the scribbles in the little red-leather notebook. Ten minutes of frowning over the late property of Nat Franz proved revealing. Apparently four other men had died in Las Vegas during the past twelve months. That year, so far as she was concerned, had been a time during which she had eaten her heart out in the pen. It was sure nice to know that dear Nat had been picking up a small fortune in blackmail mazuma. Even if he'd had to kill five guys — or at least arrange for their deaths.

Dulcie's hand closed grimly over the little book. She had enough here to send Nat Franz to the gas chamber or the electric chair. Sure it would be nice reading how Nat had been fried — or would it be gassed? Some payoff for the three-year-old frame!

But maybe there were other ways? Maybe she could make Nat smart. Maybe she could herself cut in on the lettuce he had gathered?

She stared at the notebook again, and thought it was a darned lucky break she had grabbed it out of Nat's safe. There was one entry that was very interesting. Apparently there was a guy living at Vermont Heights who was handing over hefty sums of dough to Nat. There it was nicely written out with a fine ballpoint: two entries to the tune of a mere fifteen grand. And the interesting point lay in the fact that there was no 'dead, debt cancelled' entry after the figures.

Maybe this guy was still alive, and paying. The same man would know why be was paying good dough to a ruthless hood like Nat Franz!

The man's name was Luthor Wade, and he lived at Baytree, Silver Canyon, Vermont Heights. There was even a phone number, Vermont 2179.

Dulcie sat in her auto and beat up plenty of anger at the thought of Nat Franz collecting all that money. The heel! Not content with his rake-off from the Imperial Casino, he was up to the neck in a filthy racket. She wondered why he wanted all that dough. And then she thought the guy must have a lust, a kink, an urge to seize more and more.

Some guys were like that; they never knew when to stop. You read about these things in the newspapers every day. Politicians, murderers, grafters who came to a grim end mostly because they couldn't stop somewhere on the line.

Dulcie wriggled in her seat. It was still hot although the evening had arrived. She'd had a full day. But there was time yet, she figured to call on Mr. Luthor Wade. As to the telephone — nuts! The guy wouldn't be able to see her that way!

She thought about Johnny. Now there was a nice guy; the sort of guy you could fall hard for, only he was married. She slipped the red notebook in her stocking top for safety, started the auto and tooled gently along Gilbert Avenue. Driving sedately, she rolled past Central Park, headed down Highway 63 and hit the motel at sundown.

Johnny was waiting for her, looking big, grim and sour. His dark hair crinkled over his forehead. He had taken off his coat and rolled up his shirt sleeves. His arms dangled menacingly as if he would like to beat dust out of her.

'You come back for something?' he growled.

She walked up to him with swinging hips and a smile. It was so damned simple. Her very presence was some sort of strange influence. The way she walked and smiled confounded him.

'Oh Johnny!' She made it sound like music. 'You've got to help me.' That bit was strictly teasing. 'You will won't you?' She knew he wasn't going to refuse.

'What sort of grief have you hit now?'

'Oh, nothing. It's just that I'm discovering the meaning behind Nat's gimmick. Johnny, the guy's a blackmailer and murderer! I've got him cold!'

He grabbed her roughly; felt his fingers bite through the thin dress. He was surprised at her softness under his grip. Somehow he had a mental image of her hard. He knew that didn't make sense, and he was irritated.

'Come into my cabin! What the blazes are you talking about, anyway? Get in here where you can't be overheard.'

Then they were in the cabin. He shut the door and sat beside her on the settee.

'Give!'

She told him about the visit to Randolph Greg's home. She got excited in the telling, and her blue eyes sparkled.

'Murder!' he muttered at the end of the

telling. 'Then it's for the cops.'

'I just want to see this Luthor Wade guy,' she said rapidly. 'I want to know why he's paying money to Nat. I must know. These guys would not pay up for no reason.'

'Probably the usual reasons,' interrupted Johnny. 'People get blackmailed because they have secrets, vices, things they want to hide from the world.'

'Yeah. Well, that sounds good but doesn't tell me why Martin Greg paid up. And it doesn't tell me why Luthor Wade is paying up. We can go see that guy, Johnny. Then we'll really have Nat behind the eight-ball.'

'That's all you've got in mind. Let the cops handle this — '

'Are you going with me, Johnny? Or do I go myself?'

'Okay. I'll go with you,' he decided. She smiled wickedly and seeing it, he added: 'Mainly because a gal can run into grief in the dark.'

5

Nat Franz and Ed Kibe were having a little conference. From Ed's viewpoint, Nat was in an ugly mood, pointing out that he hired Ed to do jobs for spot cash, without questions, without failures; and if he couldn't operate like that he was no use.

'It was that Johnny punk,' said Ed Kibe for the fourth time. 'I'd have got her over here, Nat. Sure I would.'

'That Johnny lobo needs medicine,' slurred Nat Franz, the memory of the uppercut to his chin still in his mind. 'I'll even with him someday.'

'I'll do that for you at a bargain price,' rapped Ed Kibe. He put his hands on the desk and looked at his dirty fingernails.

Nat Franz smoked reflectively, broodingly. 'She's left the hotel with the Johnny lug. Could be anywhere in this town. But I'll find her, I'll teach her to hold me up an' take my dough.' He was thinking maybe he ought to do this work himself because he did not want anyone to know about the red-leather notebook. Ed Kibe had failed to get Dulcie Grande back to the casino. And now Dulcie and her boyfriend had vanished. There was just that brief telephone taunt she had given him, proving she was still in town, but he hadn't been able to trace the call.

'Okay, get out and look around for those two. Look around the hotels. Ya might have some luck. Let me know if you get a break; I'd like to handle these birds myself.'

Ed Kibe nodded. 'You givin' me pay for this graft, Nat?'

'Sure, sure! It's simple work, ain't it? You scared of work or somethin'?'

'It's too simple,' sneered the other. 'You're close, Nat. You don't tell a guy much.'

'This dame took my dough — ' began Nat Franz angrily.

'Sure, I know. Ya told me. That's what I mean — ain't so often ya hand out any dope. Even now ya don't tell me much about this judy.'

Nat rose, and walked around Ed Kibe. 'If you don't like the work, beat it an' I'll get me a hustler who'll do what I want and never even ask the time of day! I don't keep guys on a payroll except legitimate workers in the casino. I hire the right guy for the right job at the right time and for the right dough. Now get out and keep your eyes wide open for that skirt and her pally. I could get a kid off the streets to do this job for candies!'

When Ed had gone. Nat drank a glass of rye and felt better. He went to his bedroom and got into evening clothes. He thought momentarily of the early days when he had bossed a gambling ring in a San Francisco cellar. Shirtsleeves had been okay in hot weather then.

Some time later, when he walked into the bar and restaurant, he looked debonair. His thin, dark hair was slicked down. He moved capably and looked dignified.

The casino was half-empty. It seemed the days of easy money were over. Now he had an additional worry. Dulcie Grande had pried into that damned notebook. He remembered vividly her taunt over the phone. ' — I'm gonna put the cops on to you and I've got a hunch it'll be the death chamber, pal.' He wished he had never made the entries in the book. A thing like that, combined with a crazy hell-bitch, was going to raise the very devil. He should have paid the skirt her ten grand at the first asking, and that would have got rid of her.

After a promenade around the restaurant, grillroom, bar and casino, he returned to his apartment in time to hear the phone ring. He picked it up, listened very carefully.

'This is Luthor Wade,' said a voice.

'Yeah? Franz speaking.'

'I've got some money for you. In small bills. I want you to come up and get it.'

Nat was silent for ten seconds. Then: 'Sure. Why not? Natch, you wouldn't have any notion of being tricky?'

'It doesn't seem to pay. You have the merit of carrying out your threats. I have read-up on the men you mention. You brutal — '

'Cut it out!' hissed Nat Franz. 'This is a

public line. Remember what I told ya. Take it easy. Okay?'

'All right,' said the other. 'I'll play ball. Come up and get your money. I hope I'm paid up now.'

'I've let you pay up in instalments,' said Nat Franz softly. 'A common business principle.'

'The other men?'

'They wouldn't pay at all.'

'The newspaper files said they were being b — er — well — pressured.'

'Newspapers are not always accurate, Mister Wade. Sure, they may have had the pressure, but they never got around to paying. That was their mistake. You know what I mean.'

'I'm realising,' said the other grimly.

'No more talk,' said Nat Franz sombrely. 'I'll be up in — say — half-an-hour. Come to your door. And be alone. If you think I'm foolin', remember those other guys.'

He put the instrument back so slowly he might have been timing the action, and looked at his watch. Time to think and then drive up to Vermont Heights.

Particularly to think, for he had not expected to hear from Luthor Wade that night.

It was satisfying to know that he intended to be sensible. A rich man's life was worth at least thirty thousand dollars. That was what Luthor Wade was paying. With other guys, it had varied. Some had handed over fifty grand before the silenced gun had forever shut them up. He had proved to his satisfaction that all the five men now dead had played the way he wanted. They had kept mighty quiet because of their fear of death. No letter, no tricks. He had picked well. That was the secret. Some victims would be obviously unsuitable. Well, he always had plenty of suckers to choose from. The casino brought many in for legitimate amusement. A gambling casino was the place to find rich men, and particularly men who feared to die. A little conversation at infrequent intervals, and he had figured out his victim.

These guys paid up simply because they were scared to die; and the screwy part was they had to die quickly because they knew too much. The fact that there were dead men added potency to threats on future suckers, as long as the future victims did not realise the men had died after paying up!

Nat Franz smiled thinly as he lit a cigarette. He had heard of Murder Incorporated; this might be the next best thing to it. The set-up was slight; he needed few hired hands. In fact, there was only himself and Billy Death.

Billy was the real goods. He was the best hired thug anyone could find. Few racketeers knew about Billy Death. The cops had nothing on him. Billy was a respectable person.

Nat Franz knew that Billy was a split personality, an out-and-out schizophrenic. He was a dangerous man if anyone whispered some instructions to him about killing. At other times, Billy Death was just a dopey youngster who liked to sit in the park and watch the birds; read comic papers and look at TV. He had a mother who lived in a crummy apartment on the east side of the town and thought Billy worked during the day and earned a lot of money. The days, however, were spent by Billy in dreaming and lazing, except on the few occasions when Nat Franz sent for him!

Nat quit thinking about the set-up. He knew one thing; this dangerous skirt, Dulcie, could upset everything. If he could get the red notebook back, he would send Billy Death along to see her, but he had to find Dulcie first.

He tied a thin scarf around his collar and, after a word to Jerry Kome, his manager, went around to the garage and got out a black sedan.

He tooled along the road, where neons threw a haze into the sky. A million signs winked at him. He thought Las Vegas was a crazy town where anything went.

The drive up to Vermont Heights did not take long. He parked his auto near Luthor Wade's house, and stared at the shape of the house. It lay well back on its landscaped lot. There was a rustle of greenery and the smell of flowers. Lights showed from a downstairs window. It was a big window of curved glass.

Nat thought it was always the same

when he had to go out and get dough like this. Always the same twinge of fear. The guy who had no nerves didn't exist. He often wondered why he had this impulse to get hold of more dough and yet more dough. The casino was losing money, sure. Yet it had made plenty in the past, and he had the black mazuma salted away. He had always been wary about it; figured it from all angles, looking for marked bills and other tricks. There hadn't been any up-to-date.

He supposed he liked dough. Gee, one of these days he'd have to spend it and get some fun! He walked up the driveway and stabbed the bell. The next moment the door opened and a guy stood there. The opening door and the man's flashing hands were simultaneous movements. A gun prodded Nat's chest.

'Come right in!' said Johnny Lebaron.

6

Nat stared. He had expected resentment and a few bitter words from Luthor Wade — not the sight of this big lug.

Johnny took hold of his lapel and pulled him into the hall, while Dulcie closed the door. Luthor Wade was standing at the foot of the stairs, a grim little man with rimless spectacles and a rather lost look.

'We were right behind Mr. Wade when he phoned you, Nat,' Johnny began. 'He could send you to the gas chamber overnight!'

There was a clamminess on Nat's forehead. He hardly knew why he walked in with the others into a room, but he did. His brain started to work, recovering from the shock of the unexpected. He realised he was trapped.

'You swine! You tricky devil!' Luthor Wade burst out. 'Now I know you killed those men after they paid up! You probably planned death for me. You wanted the full sum of money first!'

'That seems to be the setup,' commented Johnny. It was a long time since he had used a gun, but he kept the Smith and Wesson trained nicely on Nat Franz. 'Now we know why the victims paid up. We can guess it was the same as the way you handled Mr. Wade. It was simply pay-up-or-die. You told them about some guys who had died as if they had been killed because they refused to pay. And it wasn't that way at all. You killed them off after you got the dough. Then used their deaths as a threat to the next poor devil. Well, Nat, you're on the spot now.'

Nat Franz found his tongue.

'Wade, you're making a big mistake listening to these fools. Ring for the cops! You'll die just the same.'

'That's a stupid bluff,' snapped Johnny.

'Don't listen to 'em, Wade. I didn't kill any of those guys. I've got a gunny who does that job, and you're lined up, unless I see this gunny an' talk to him. An' I can't do that if the cops get me.'

Luthor Wade began to shake. Nat

smiled thinly, and helped things along with more insinuating threats.

'Sure, I could be in the jail-house, Wade. But you could be on the end of a gat at the same time. You'd never know when the slug would take you — '

'Shut up!' shrieked Luthor Wade. He was trembling, his eyes wide pools behind the glinting glasses.

'Don't fall for that spiel,' grated Johnny. 'This guy can't touch you once the cops stick him in the cell. That's the slimiest bluff I've ever heard!'

Johnny Lebaron lifted the phone. His hand was slammed down again by Luthor Wade who leaped fonward.

'No! Let me think!'

'Okay, think!' snapped Johnny. 'Just think that this guy had you lined up for death even if you paid. You thought you were buying your life if you paid up. Well, you were buying death. A guy who can put on a double-cross like that can't be trusted. So don't believe this phooey about stoppin' the killer. If this gink gets out of here, he's going to have us all killed because we know too much!'

During the time that Johnny and Dulcie had talked to Luthor before Nat's arrival he had been calm and collected, but now he had lost his nerve. He looked wildly from Nat Franz to Johnny. 'But — but — maybe it's true! Maybe this madman will kill me!'

'Nuts! Look — '

'Let's make a deal,' insinuated Nat Franz. 'I guarantee you your life, Wade, if you shut your trap about me from now on.'

'A deal? Yes, yes. A deal! I — '

'You're crazy,' growled Johnny. 'He'll kill you as quick as a rattler can strike. Anyway, Wade, you don't make the decision any more. I'm going to phone the cops.'

His hand fell to the instrument once again. Nat Franz made a swift appeal to Dulcie Grande.

'Don't let him phone! I can pay you two big dough for a getaway.'

Johnny rested his hand on the black phone. 'And what do we get? A slug from a silenced gat?'

Dulcie moved a step and stared at the racketeer. The sudden offer confused her.

She had retained a fixed notion of making Nat Franz suffer for the three years she had spent in the pen; now he was offering her big dough. Maybe he would pay big dough, too.

Johnny watched her narrowly. 'He's got you going now! Hell, this gink sure understands his people! Wonder if he understands me?' He swung back to Nat Franz. 'How about making me an offer, too? Go ahead. Every guy has his price, hasn't he? What's mine, Nat? A hundred bucks — or a million?'

'I could hand you plenty. Look. You've got the edge on me, but it could be worth dough to you. Just give me that notebook and let me beat it. Or keep the notebook and come with me until ya get your dough As for Mr. Wade, as long as he keeps away from cops, he'll live. I can arrange that. I can arrange anything with my gunny. What d'ya say?'

'If you want my considered opinion. Nat,' remarked Johnny Lebaron, 'I figure you're the world's trickiest louse!'

Luthor Wade's contribution was a choking sound.

Jonny lifted the phone. He stuck a finger in the dial. He had to lower the gun to achieve this.

Dulcie said: 'I'll hold the gun for you, Johnny.'

He nodded, handed the weapon over. He figured she knew how to handle it since the gun had originally belonged to her.

She took the heater and held it steadily for a second. Johnny Lebaron dialled another number. Nat Franz was showing his dentures in a desperate twist of his lips. Luthor Wade was still choking and dithering.

'Don't dial any more, Johnny!' snapped Dulcie.

He looked up and saw the gun pointing at him. He gave it a second stare and then said: 'Point it at Nat, you fool.'

'Don't you get it?' she spat. 'I'm taking up on Nat's offer. I have the notebook. I guess that's more evidence than any amount of talk, and that's what he wants.' She swung her head, making her blonde hair dance gaily. 'Look, Nat, we're making a deal. Strictly for dough because I still hate you!'

Nat Franz moved swiftly around to her. He got close to her side in one movement. Johnny was the man on the end of the gun.

'You goddam fool!' Johnny made an involuntary movement. Then he stopped because she steadied the gun resentfully. 'He'll trick you.'

'I want dough,' she said, but privately she was thinking she, too, could work some tricks after she got dough out of Nat Franz.

'All right, let's get out!' snapped Nat. 'Quit the gum-beating. We can make a deal, sure.'

He began to edge to the door. Dulcie moved with him.

Johnny looked at the gun.

'You wouldn't shoot me.'

'Don't try me, Johnny. Don't try me.' She laughed bitterly. 'I don't even know what I might do myself!'

He gave a disgusted laugh and stepped forward. Then the next moment he had to contend with a clinging figure that panted words:

'Don't send that gunman to me, Franz!

I'm helping you! You can get away now. You'll remember this is a deal!'

Johnny struggled with Luthor Wade. The man clung to his arms and legs, obstructing him and sobbing out his terror. By the time Johnny was able to throw the man to one side. Dulcie and Nat Franz had vanished down the passage and out into the night. He heard a car engine purr loudly and then the grate of gears as they were engaged too quickly. He knew Dulcie was driving off.

'You reckless, greedy little fool!' he bawled into the night. 'You'll be a corpse by morning!'

He stamped back to the lounge of Luthor Wade's home, realising that he couldn't phone the cops. Nat Franz would be stampeded to violent action with cops looking for him. He'd turn the tables on the girl. Played slower, there was a chance that Dulcie might be able to handle him.

'One tricky devil against another!' snarled Johnny.

He stared at Luthor Wade. The man was shakily pouring himself a glass of whisky. His face was just the imprint for a mighty sick guy.

'Hell, I'm in this to my neck!' Johnny stamped around the room, muttering aloud. 'I'll have to find Dulcie and help her. I can't see her become a lovely corpse. Did I come three thousand miles for this? Did I leave a possessive wife and her damned relations to hook up with a crazy, painted bitch? I'm going,' he snapped at Luthor Wade. 'Don't phone the cops. Take a tip. Get a night plane to Mexico, Florida or hell-knows where. Then you'll be safe.'

He strode out of the house, hit the brightly-lit street and clambered aboard a bus. He was deposited in the heart of Las Vegas less than ten minutes later, and entered the Imperial Casino. He went through the restaurant, and then the gaming rooms, but there was no sign of Nat Franz. He remembered the hood who called himself Ed Kibe, and wondered if he would be around, but there were only waiters, barmen and croupiers. From the direction of the gaming rooms came the click of roulette wheels. A smattering of people were in there, and another group at the bar. The joint wasn't exactly hectic.

Johnny got tired of hanging around. He made his way across the room; found the passage that led to Nat's apartment at the back of the place and opened the door marked PRIVATE. He eased a hand to the glass door at the other side of the little lobby. Then he slid it open and stared around the room.

There was a woman in the room, but no one else. She was a dark-haired woman of about thirty with sharp eyes that held Johnny up for questioning.

'I'm lookin' for Nat Franz.' he said. 'Have you seen him?'

She smoothed her long evening dress. 'I usually see him, but he isn't here.' She nearly made it 'ain't'.

Johnny said: 'Yeah?'

'I won't wait much longer for him,' she said.

'Me too,' said Johnny. 'How long have you been waiting?'

'Half-an-hour and more. What's it to you? I haven't seen you before.'

'Johnny Lebaron is the name. Nope you haven't seen me around.'

'I thought I knew all Nat's friends!' She seemed suspicious.

'I'm a new one,' rapped Johnny. 'What's your name?'

'Emma Blaine — what's it to you?'

'Baby, I don't know.' He walked across the room and looked into the office where the steel safe squatted in its corner. He thought it probably held more secrets, and remembering the combination number, turned the dial to the first numeral. Then to the next and so on. He was quite surprised when the door opened at the end of the combination. So Nat had not changed the arrangement!

'Say, what are you doing in there!' hissed a frightened voice. He looked up at Emma Blaine's shocked face.

'Siddown!' snapped Johnny. He pulled her into the office and slammed the door shut. 'Don't start yelling,' he warned, 'or you might get hurt.'

He watched her for a moment and then turned the key in the lock, pocketed it, and went back to the safe.

He pulled out the trays and went through the contents. He didn't know what he would find but he wanted Nat's secrets: preferably the sort of secrets that would gas the guy.

He did not find another red notebook. He saw plenty of small ledgers and guessed they contained accounts of the casino. There was a wad of money. A pile of bills lay clipped together. He found pass-books for three different banks. But it was the photograph that interested him and made him pause longest.

It was a good print on 4 X 4 paper. He looked at the photograph of a young guy in slack sports trousers and a shirt. He had clear-cut features and seemed about twenty-five years old. On the other side of the print was written:

'Billy Death seems bored. Must give my gunny some more work to do. Incredible that fate gave him such an appropriate name.'

Johnny recognised Nat Franz's handwriting. It was the same as the scrawl in the red notebook, and done with the same pen and ink. He shoved the safe contents back and swung the silent door, then slipped the photograph into his pocket and returned to Emma Blaine.

'You don't know it,' he said convincingly, 'but I'm a detective from Police Headquarters. If you don't want to get into real bad trouble, just shut up about me going into Nat's safe. Now let's get out of here.'

He opened the office door and left the key in the lock.

They walked into the lounge. The woman, who was obviously not the moll type, looked ready to faint.

Johnny had reached the door when he heard the sound of the outer door being opened and saw a shadow looming on the other side of the glass.

He backed away, flattening himself against a convenient wall. Then Nat Franz walked into the room. Johnny sprang and gripped his arms from behind. He held him so firmly the man was bent like a bow.

'Where's Dulcie?'

'You fool — she's — just — left me!'

'Yeah?'

'She got her dough! We made a deal!'

'Yeah,' said Johnny again. 'Give it me straight, you lyin' swine. What happened to Dulcie?'

7

Dulcie Grande sat on a chair in an abandoned shack on the outskirts of Las Vegas with hands tied behind her back and her slender legs trussed together. There was every chance that her nylons were due to be ruined.

Billy Death, the young man who stared at her with long curiosity, was eating an apple. He also had a comic book sticking out of his shirt pocket.

Dulcie was not gagged. She would have screamed to high heaven if she thought her yells would be heard; but she had known it was useless from the start. The shack to which Nat had taken her lay on the fringe of a desolate brickyard. She had seen that when Nat had driven her auto there.

She had not gone willingly. Hell, no; Nat had tricked her minutes after leaving Johnny Lebaron at Luthor Wade's house. Just to think of it again filled her with fury. The slob had distracted her attention, seized her gun, and demanded the notebook. She'd tried to bluff. He had searched her handbag, and from then on it was only a step to searching her. He had found the little red-leather notebook, taken her straight to this cabin and trussed her up. She had had a real scare more than once that he was going to kill her on the spot. He had driven with one hand and kept a gun in her side. She could have fought him while he was binding her, but the gun scared her. She had thought he would trigger at any moment if she fought.

Then he had left her and returned later with this pasty-faced punk, giving him orders that she was to be watched

'I want to use her to get a guy. After that, Billy, they're your meat — but not until I say so, Billy! Not until I say so!'

Dulcie watched the punk. She thought he was young but not too young to be uninterested in a pretty girl. She had to use anything to get out of this mess. She guessed Nat Franz was thinking of trapping Johnny Lebaron. Bitterly, she realised that she was a fool, and Johnny had been right. Nat was the world's slimiest trickster, and she was no match. She should have sent the slob to the cops when she had the chance.

The crunch of Billy's white teeth, biting into the apple jerked her thoughts back to the punk. Nat had been gone about five minutes. She started: 'Say, Billy, you don't want to have any truck with a crook like Nat Franz. He'll get you into trouble with the cops.'

Billy Death munched steadily at his apple. A clock would have ticked off many seconds before he replied slowly: 'Nat's a great guy.'

'Let me go, Billy,' Dulcie whispered. 'You ever had a girlfriend, Billy? Ever kissed a girl? You wouldn't like to see your girl tied up, would you?'

She saw his soft, white face looking at her curiously as if she were some kind of an exhibit. 'He's going to kill me, Billy!' she wailed. 'D'you hear? Kill me!'

Billy Death stared mournfully. His pale blue eyes looked right through her. Slowly, he lowered his hand and dropped the apple on the shack floor. He was staring in fascination at her as if he saw something terrible. He swayed a little but was perfectly balanced. Then he turned slowly and walked back to the other side of the shack with his head down.

'No!' he muttered. 'Nat's a great guy. He won't kill you. Not Nat!'

'But he will!' Dulcie wailed again. 'Get me out of here. Billy! Get me out! I'll give you money.' And then she paused, remembering that Nat Franz had taken the ten grand off her. That had been a bitter blow, but it was secondary to the fact that her life was now in danger. 'I'll give you money, Billy,' she repeated wildly. Any ruse was good enough if it got her out of this jam.

'I don't want money from you,' muttered Billy.

He slouched around the shack, hands shoved into his trouser pockets and kicked at some rubbish lying on the hard-earth floor.

'Look, Billy, you couldn't do this to a girl!' she panted. 'Billy — you're a nice feller, get me out of here. Be a nice guy!'

He raised his head and gave her that stare of curiosity again. 'My name ain't just Billy.'

'No?' she encouraged.

'I'm Billy Death.'

The reply was soft, normal, but there was something else. Dulcie wasn't analysing anything.

'You — you — ' She groped for a sane reply.

He smiled sleepily and walked around the shack again, a slim, slouching figure with no hint of the fact that he was a nerveless killer, capable of using a silenced gun with accuracy and slipping away unseen, unheard.

Dulcie realised that she had been a complete fool. If she had taken Johnny Lebaron's advice, Nat Franz would have been in the cell by now. The cops would have acted because Las Vegas cops must have seen similarities behind the deaths of five men. She would have retained her ten grand, and seen Nat on his way to hell. She had lost all that. Pretty soon she might even lose her life.

She struggled with the ropes binding

her hands behind her back. It was an agonising, futile effort. She hadn't the strength for tricks like that. She had no more chance of getting free than a wretched dog due for drowning with the aid of four bricks around its neck!

She prayed for a miracle. With every minute, her nerves were getting as ragged as a frayed hawser. The time dragged on like some horrifying, turgid stream.

The sound that shattered came suddenly. The shack door burst open, its shaky wood tearing inwards as if under the impact of exploding gunpowder. Two men appeared.

Dulcie shrieked: 'Johnny!'

He slammed Nat Franz to the floor and lashed at Billy Death, his fists ramming out with wicked efficiency. Billy's reactions were too slow; maybe he wasn't cut out for the rough stuff. It seemed that way because he collapsed against the shack wall without putting his hands up. Johnny pulled him off and repeated the treatment until he collapsed like a lifeless dummy, then whirled on Nat Franz as he tried to get to his feet. A smashing blow flung him back to the ground. Johnny brought out the Smith & Wesson and pointed it at him. 'Stick close to the floor, pal!'

He strode over to Dulcie and released her, then, remembering the photograph, spent a few seconds staring sombrely at Billy Death. If he was a gunny he certainly did not look one. He stepped over and frisked him, but there was no gun. Queer, but good enough. No gun, no trouble.

Dulcie came out in a rush of words, 'Johnny, you're a pal! I knew you'd get me out of this!'

'I don't know how the hell you knew that,' grunted Johnny. 'You're one lucky dame who could be so dead! I had to hammer the truth out of Nat. When I found he had the Smith & Wesson, I knew he'd tricked you. Hell, that heater certainly gets around.'

'Where's my ten grand?' Dulcie blazed suddenly, wheeling on Nat.

The man was looking mighty sick. He hadn't taken that sort of drubbing for a long time.

Dulcie got down beside him and

slapped his face. Nat snarled, raised a hand. He saw Johnny's gesture with the gun and his hand sank again. Dulcie thrust snatching fingers into his inside pocket and whipped out a wide billfold stuffed with her money. She snatched the wad out and tossed the billfold back to Nat Franz. 'Where's the red notebook?'

Nat raised his head; forced a grin over his sour face. 'Where ya won't find it, bitch!'

'You've hidden it?'

He snarled triumphantly: 'Nope. After I left ya here, I stopped your auto for five minutes an' tore that blasted notebook into bits. I even sliced up the covers! Then I drove on and let the bits fly to the wind. They must be all over three square miles of back streets by now — nice little bits no bigger than confetti!'

Dulcie made a savage gesture with her hand. 'Maybe he's lying?'

'Maybe,' said Johnny. 'But maybe not.' He came closer to Nat. 'You wouldn't be kiddin', would you? I'd like to find that notebook because I'd like to hand it over to the cops. Strictly no funny business about you buyin' it back. So where is it, pal? Give it straight.'

'I've told ya! In a million little bits in a million different corners of this town.'

Johnny looked Nat over warily, unsmilingly. Then he bent down and patted his pockets. There was no bulky feel of a book. But he did find a tiny fragment of paper in one of his pockets.

'Sure looks like a bit out of a notebook. Got a red line through it. Could be you're talking the truth, pal.'

'You can look around the streets,' sneered Nat. 'Maybe you'll find one or two more bits. You'll be real smart if ya can get enough to stick together.'

Dulcie jumped up, her dress swinging. 'You mean it's true, Johnny?'

'Guess we've got to hand it to him. It was a smart move. That notebook is the only thing the cops could use as evidence. Maybe we could tell them — '

'Ya can't do anything to me,' said Nat thickly. He rose slowly to his feet and dusted his clothes. 'Ya couldn't go to the cops with a screwball tale like that. I ain't got a police record. I'm a respectable owner of a licensed casino in this town an' I pay taxes. You're just two crazy fools! A dame with a record — an' you. Who the hell are ya, anyway?'

'Johnny Lebaron, feller, And I don't like your talk.'

'Sure, sure!' Nat's sneer was so thick one could have scraped filth from it. 'So ya're Johnny Lebaron. Well, the hell with ya. You can't do anything to me.'

Dulcie glared at Nat and clutched the wad of paper money. Johnny was thinking maybe Nat was right about Dulcie not being able to approach the police — particularly with her record. So far as he was concerned he wasn't a crook and didn't intend to become one, although the present set-up had him heading that way. Anyone who got the notion that crime paid was as crazy as hell. It was a sure path to dirt and death.

He moved the gun up and pointed it at Nat's paunch. 'You've got a smart murder set-up, and I guess you're itching to put your gunnies on to Dulcie and me before we open our mouths too wide. Nothing doing, pal. You and Billy are coming along with me.'

8

The shack was deserted. Outside, in Dulcie's auto, Johnny held a gun trained on Nat Franz and Billy Death. He saw no reason to put them back into circulation just so they could plot another little murder fest, involving a guy and a gal. Yet, finding an alternative was difficult. Had the red notebook still existed he could have turned them over to the cops, but without it he felt dubious about this course.

'What proof have we?' he muttered to Dulcie. 'And I mean proof.'

'Luthor Wade — ' she began.

'Nuts! That guy's too scared to talk.' Johnny was sitting in a half-turned position with the gun pointing firmly at Nat Franz and Billy. Dulcie was at the wheel. A good way off the neons of central Las Vegas threw a haze into the sky.

Dulcie gave an excited laugh. 'I know

who could bust Nat high, wide and handsome! Billy Death! Isn't he the gunny? I bet you we could make him talk.'

Johnny nodded reflectively. 'That's the best idea you've dreamed up for some time. Get a confession from this feller and maybe it's as good as the red notebook. If the cops can't pin something on Nat with a confession from Billy Death, they should be fired and the chimps from the local zoo stuck at their desks! But how do we start getting a confession from this lunkhead, honey?'

'Well, we've got to get him away from here.'

'Yeah. That goes for the two of them. Take only Billy, and Nat would be all hot-panted to get another killer damned fast — with probably the three of us as targets.'

'We have the auto. We could get out of Las Vegas.' She looked at him expectantly.

'Okay.' He nodded. 'Let's get a hideout, baby. Move this heap and head out.'

She needed no second telling, and tooled out of the desolate old brickyard.

Passing the gaunt heaps of old bricks and kilns, gave her feverish ideas of what she could do to Nat Franz. Why, she could brick the guy up and leave him until he confessed and wrote the thing out into the bargain! There were many things the old site suggested to her. She was convinced that torture was the only way in which confessions could be extracted. She thought she could put over that sort of play.

The auto rolled on to the highway and surged to higher speeds. She did not know Las Vegas county very well, but she got on to a highway which sliced out into the wastelands, swooping across land which had once been traversed by prospector and burro.

After five miles of the slashing highway, the glitter of a Chevron Gas Station loomed up. She began to slow down. 'Have to pull in for gas.'

Johnny twisted around and got a new bead on Nat Franz and his gunny.

'You guys wouldn't be thinking of playin' it tricky, now, would you? Better keep quiet.'

'Or what?' sneered Nat.

'Or I plant a slug in you, maybe.'

'Maybe!' Nat was leering.

'Yeah, maybe. Then Dulcie will step on the gas pedal an' get away. You gonna chance it?'

They got the gas tank filled, Johnny sat and stared at Nat and Billy. He improvised a little trick of holding the gun under one arm, just under his armpit. The gas attendant didn't notice. Dulcie paid and got the auto rolling again.

Johnny relaxed when she built up speed with the headlights hollowing out a tunnel of light ahead.

'You're crazy,' Nat breathed eventually. 'Billy won't talk. He's a queer guy. You could stick pins in him and he wouldn't blink.'

'And you?' asked Johnny conversationally.

'I'm certainly not signing anythin' that puts me in the cell.'

'Guess we'll see.' Johnny lit a cigarette and almost ate the smoke. He hadn't fired a cigarette for some time. 'You want to know somethin', Nat? I'm a guy at a loose end right now. You don't know much about me, except my name, and you never will — from me, anyway. Being at a loose end, I figure I might as well do something useful with my time. Up-to-date it's been a bit hazy. I've helled around because I've been pushed by you and Dulcie. I think that'll stop. Maybe that's optimistic. Let's say it ought to stop. We're going to push you around now. It'll end when we hand you over to the cops on a platter — you and that lunkhead.'

Eventually, as time and the auto sped on, silence fell on the group. Dulcie concentrated on driving. Johnny kept a wary eye on the two birds in the rear seating. He thought they would be crazy to try anything tricky with the car swooping along at speed most of the time, but you never knew.

He was quite happy. Las Vegas or this desert lands were all the same to him. Sooner or later they would find the right place to stop.

They did find it. About thirty minutes

later they passed some shanties standing on a ridge of hills half a mile off the road. The moonlight showed them up as purple shadows on the ridge.

'Not even a roof!' remarked Johnny, 'But who wants a roof in Nevada in summertime?'

Dulcie stopped the auto. Johnny made swift gestures with the gun, motioning the two killers to get out of the car.

'The end of the line, pals.'

Minutes later, as they walked around the site, he made another discovery. The place was the site of an old silver mine, for a weather-beaten board, scoured by winter rains and sand-storms, bore a legend: ATLAS SILVER MINING.

A shaft went deep into the hillside. There was plenty of uninviting darkness at the mouth, but Johnny got the idea it was just the place for Nat and Billy Death. It was a sure thing they were not going to be taken to some plush residence. The worse the hideout was, the better.

Johnny kept behind the two men in case they got one of those screwy ideas that a pair of legs can beat a bullet. He wondered if he would shoot. Apparently Nat Franz and Billy Death thought he might. His earlier threat seemed to have some effect. Men who had lived with the sound of their own guns as incidental music apparently didn't like to hear others go off!

'Get the auto up here, Dulcie.' Johnny ordered. 'I want to have some light in this cave. Then we can walk in. Sure would be too bad if we fell down a hole.'

'What about the shanties?'

'Nope. Come daylight you'll be able to see through those ruins.'

She drove the auto up close to the hillside and parked it so that the head-lights plunged into the cave mouth. Johnny walked his prisoners in and they went down a tunnel almost large enough to take the car.

The shaft had a sandy bed where sand had blown in during many storms. After going about thirty yards down the shaft, Johnny ordered his two prisoners to halt.

'Squat down and don't get tricky.' Dulcie was behind him. He half-turned and said; 'You got any adhesive tape in your auto tool kit?'

'Yes. I guess so. When I got the car the mech said it had everything.'

'Okay. Get it. I can bind these ginks nicely. That's the first job. After that we — ' He whipped around again, hearing the sounds of Nat and Billy rushing into headlong flight. He saw them, dark shapes plunging down the shaft!

9

Johnny raised the gun, but he had to overcome a repugnance to shoot a man, and that slowed him. Then, with a curse, he did trigger. The gun kicked in his hand, and the explosion sounded deafening in the shaft.

The auto headlights thinned at this part of the tunnel.

They were thirty yards down. As he fired the gun, Johnny jerked forward. He got a photographic glimpse of the two running men and then they seemed to dive sideways and disappear.

He reached the spot where they had vanished some seconds later. He saw a tunnel branching off the main shaft. It was really dark. He realised he could not shoot in pitch blackness. He couldn't see anything. He halted, listened intently and heard dull noises that he could not position. Then Dulcie reached his side. He glanced at her, saw her startled face in the thin residue of light that penetrated this part of the shaft.

'They've gone,' he jerked. 'And I didn't hit them. You'd better beat it back to the auto. You might get lost in this damned tunnel. Seems to be a number of shafts.'

She clutched his arm. 'Johnny, be careful! What if you get lost?'

'Baby. Don't tell me you're startin' to worry! Get back to the auto. I'm going after those two guys.'

He shook her hand off and thrust into the branch shaft. The darkness closed on him like water around a falling stone. He slowed, went on with outstretched hands and nerves as taut as a hunted animal. He realised he could be walking into a trap. Sure, he had a gun, but he couldn't see. He was a blind guy with a gun. He wondered if that made sense.

As he moved, fragments of rock fell from the roof. Some chips hit him while other bits fell just ahead of him. He thought it would be cute if the roof suddenly fell. That could happen if he used the gun. These old shafts were usually on the verge of collapse.

He halted, listened for further sounds of the two men, but there was just the ominous tinkle of loose rock chips. Where had the two guys gone? Had they fallen into a pit?

Sweat dripped down his face. The shaft was narrower. His own breath seemed to rebound into his face again. There was a suffocating feeling. Thinking about sudden pits in the shaft door slowed him. Hell, he didn't want to end up a broken mess of limbs. He halted again and, listening carefully, presently heard something breathing.

The next moment shapes sprang at him. His gun stayed in his pocket and he was given no time to use it. He was struggling with two men, warding off fists that sought to smash viciously into his face. He threw one man back with a punch that clipped him solidly on the side of the face. For a swing in the dark it was good. He heard a thud as the man hit the shaft wall, then dust and chips slithered down. The other man was gripping Johnny's arm. He knew that it was Nat Franz. Then he swung a fist that could have knocked a hole in a wall, but, instead, connected with Nat's body and sent him staggering backwards.

There was no respite. Johnny had his back to the cave wall and figured to keep it that way. A shape blundered up, located him, and then a chunk of rock crashed into fragments inches from his head. Johnny grimaced, screwing up his eyes, at the same time flinging out a scooping fist that connected with Billy Death's head. The gunny staggered back.

Johnny moved away from the wall, determined to get at least one of these men. He heard movements near him and by some sort of instinct closed with Nat Franz. Nat, armed with a lump of rock, tried for Johnny's face but missed and connected with his head.

Dullness swam into Johnny's brain. He had only one thought, and that was to hang on to his attacker. He clung like a load of pliable lead. Nat couldn't use the rock again. The mists slowly receded from Johnny's mind and allowed him to use the strength of his arms, body and legs.

He rammed Nat against the shaft wall,

thrusting his hands against the rasping rock, so that he was forced to drop the chunk of stone. Johnny jabbed a punch to his chin that weakened him. Getting a hold on him was easy after that and Johnny pushed him back along the tunnel. They went about three yards, and then Nat struggled afresh.

Johnny, aided by a burst of fury, got the man further along the shaft. He could have pulled out his gun and used it as a threat, but he didn't. He thought he would show that slob he could handle him. He fought and stumbled on until finally he reached a branch where the faint glow from the auto headlights filtered along. He turned right and sent Nat staggering on with a jab to the kidneys, wondering where Billy Death was.

When they reached the shaft mouth Johnny whipped out his gun and rammed it into Nat's side. 'I'm sick of you! If I shot you, it would be the easy way out!'

Nat ceased struggling. He stood and gulped at clean night air. 'What's all this gettin' ya, Lebaron? Ya must be crazy! I won't come gunnin' for ya, if ya let me go!'

'Shut up.'

'I tell ya — '

'You're a killer!' snarled Johnny. 'You an' that gunny, Billy Death. I'm going to hand you over to the cops with a ticket on you that says what you are. I'm — hell!'

A sound like the rumble of a locomotive in a tunnel came from the old silver mine working. The dull noise of falling rock lasted for some seconds. Johnny, Dulcie and Nat Franz turned and stared. The auto headlights bored into the shaft mouth. The hillside rose in a gaunt shape. As the sound of the falling rock died away, Johnny said: 'Seems like a lot of stone came down. I don't see Billy Death.'

He turned again. 'Get that adhesive tape, Dulcie. Let's tie this bird up and then I'll take another looksee into that shaft.'

Dulcie ran to the auto, looked in the tool-kit. A minute later Nat Franz was sitting down with his hands taped behind his back and his ankles neatly bound.

Johnny stared at the shaft. 'No sign of the gunny.'

Dulcie shrieked: 'Don't go in there again!'

'I've got to see what's happened to that gunny,' Johnny called back. 'Keep those lights on.'

He penetrated down the shaft and turned the corner. The darkness welcomed him back. It was like a soft, black cloak falling around him. He didn't like the feeling.

He had hardly gone ten yards when he stumbled into a pile-up of rock. He felt all around it. So far as he could see the roof had collapsed, filling the shaft. He certainly could not get past that fall. If Billy Death was under that this was surely the end. If he was beyond the fall, then he was buried alive.

Johnny turned and stumbled back to the light from the auto. He walked out of the shaft and found an armful of woman wrapping slender arms around his neck. Their kiss started softly, but soon it was intense.

'Now look, baby — ' he breathed.

'Oh, gee, I'm so glad to see you!'

'Look, baby, there's been a fall of roof in there and the way is blocked. Maybe that Billy Death guy is dead and maybe he's not. Either way I don't see what I can do about it.'

'Oh. Johnny, let's get away from here. I don't like it!'

'You can say that again! But we'll squat in one of the shanties until sunup. When we head back to Las Vegas, we want a confession from Nat.'

'Think he'll give it?'

'Maybe. If he doesn't, he can stay here until he rots.'

That was strictly bluff for Nat Franz to hear. The man sat dejectedly. He had heard enough about Billy Death, but he had not spoken.

Johnny inspected a shanty. It wasn't too bad. It would do to hold Nat Franz, anyway. He went back to the man and carried him to the shanty. 'You're lucky. If the damned shack falls on you it won't hurt much because the timber is just about rotten with termites and weather. You won't be like Billy Death. Could be your gunny is dead, Nat. How'd you feel about that?'

'I don't feel anythin'. Get smart, Lebaron. I'm not signing any confession.'

'Okay. We've got plenty of time. You might be glad to make a statement when you've been left without water or food. Figure it out, Nat. Even if the cops had a signed confession from you, a good lawyer could prove how it was obtained. Maybe that would make it invalid. So that's your gamble, Nat. We'll see how it goes, huh?'

10

Johnny slid out of the auto as the first rays of sun clawed into the sky. He looked back at Dulcie, still asleep, and thought she was a strange kid, so much mixed-up.

With the return of daylight, the landscape could be ascertained. The shanties and the silver mine drift were close to a hillside. All around was flat, semi-arid land and not so far away the straight concrete strip of highway. As Johnny glanced around, he saw trucks flying along the road at top speed. The drivers, he figured, would be too busy to notice much.

He lit a cigarette and walked over to the shanty. He looked in and jarred to a halt as if suddenly turned to stone. Nat Franz had gone.

Strips of discarded adhesive tape lying on the earth floor of the shack told only part of the story. Johnny crinkled his face in disbelief. How in the name of everything could a guy get out of that sort of binding? Twisted adhesive tape had plenty of strength. The knots that had been made had been good.

Johnny eased out his gun, and turned around. He walked swiftly through the other shanties, noted the remains of old machinery but nothing else. He strode over to the shaft mouth, and stared down. Nothing but a confused pattern of footprints in the sandy bed met his gaze. He walked back to the shanty that had held Nat Franz. He stared at the footprints there. They hardly made sense. They were churned up, and he wasn't a Navajo Indian.

He uttered a little snort which might have been a laugh had there been anything funny in the setup. He didn't see anything funny. It struck him that the potentialities of the hell-around were not over.

He wakened Dulcie. He had to walk around with a gun in his hand. He had to move his head fast at every sound, real or imaginary. He even watched the speeding trucks on the highway. He thought if Nat was really a big shot crook, he ought to have a truck-load of hoods tearing up with gun, rifles and dynamite just so that there could be a real shindig. Apparently Nat wasn't doing it that way. In fact, Nat wasn't that sort of guy at all.

When Dulcie rubbed the sleep out of her eyes and slid out of the car, he told her but good. 'Nat's gone, honey, and I don't like it.'

The news wakened her if nothing else. She had to run to the shanty and have a look.

'Gone!' She came back to him. 'Gee, he could have killed us! While we were asleep!'

'I wasn't asleep — not all the time, anyway. Seems like he was able to slink away without us seein' him. Probably he figured I'd shoot if he tackled me. Yep, he's gone, sugar. And that's that!'

'No it isn't!' she snapped. 'Get into the auto. We're going back to L.V.'

'I thought you'd say that.' His grey eyes were quizzical.

'We can't let him get away with it — ' she began.

'Sure, sure, but any further contacts with Nat Franz will be like stroking a black mamba. Okay. Let's go back to L.V. Let's go back to the motel and get our bags. I feel mussed.'

'You do? Say, Mister, I feel awful hungry, too.'

'You look nice, just the same,' he assured her.

She gave him a long, smiling glance. 'Did you ever say that to your wife? You wouldn't have left her if you were in the habit of saying that to her.'

He jammed his hands into his pockets. 'It was like that at first with me, but never with her. I guess I was just a possession. Funny — wasn't other men or women that got into our life. Just coldness. Coldness isn't life, baby. You can't do anythin' with the cold.'

They got into the auto. Johnny stuck the keys in the dash and got the engine firing. They jolted over the wasteland. Then they rolled on to the highway and headed back east. Soon the tyres were zipping on hot pavement.

Dulcie began to get critical of her

appearance. 'Gee, look at my stockings! And my dress! Say, I'll need something new. And I'll have to bank this ten grand.'

'Best place for it. If Nat gets it again, you'll have lost it. But I guess Nat may have grimmer things to think about.'

He drove into downtown Las Vegas a good bit later, when the streets were thronged with early morning shoppers. It seemed incredible to imagine that he had been in the town only twenty-four hours.

He drove along Centuria Avenue, passing the City Hall that bore a distant resemblance to chrome-and-plush night-joints, then down one of the freeways and out of town to the motel on the border.

Some time was spent by Dulcie and Johnny in cleaning, washing and eating. They finished breakfast in the motel restaurant. Johnny had gotten into new worsted trousers, a clean dark blue shirt with necktie to match and a rayon jacket. The gun made an unpleasant bulge in the jacket pocket.

Dulcie thought he looked nice when newly-shaved and smelling of pine hair cream. She was fresh and attractive in a soft white dress that had apparently been made from a mould of her. There was a dash of red at the waist, and it matched the ton of stuff she wore on her lips. Dulcie certainly went to town with her lipstick.

They drove into town later in the day. He wasn't worrying about Nat Franz. For two pins, he could forget the guy. For less than that, he could get quite reckless over Dulcie Grande.

They parked the auto in a two-tier lot while Dulcie went into a branch of the Associated Bank and stashed the ten grand. She showed Johnny her book. 'Gee, I'm rich. You want a beer, Mister? Or a Colonel Lucas highball? Let's go buy something wet and cool.'

'It's your lettuce,' he grinned. 'Now me, I've only got about eight hundred bucks, and if I want any more I'll have to contact my bank. Doris will sure find out after that.'

'Why? How?'

'Her Pop happens to be president of the bank.'

A bit later they were in *Maraco's Bar*,

which is on Sixth Street and very nice, too. It was full of women, looking very lonely. They were getting divorces and had to stick six weeks in the town.

Surrounded by ornamental glass, tubbed palms, chrome and red plush, Johnny and Dulcie did not notice Emma Blaine among all the other women. After the first sharp glance, Emma sidled out of the room and went to a telephone in the cool foyer, with the result that when Johnny and Dulcie left the place a man called Ed Kibe followed them at a discreet distance.

He was working to Nat's instructions and he expected dough, but he was anticipating some enjoyment from his work because he had not forgotten how Johnny Lebaron had hit him. He carried a gun. He had used a heater more than once and killed men. He had always killed for money, which is worse than killing in a frenzy of temper. He had forgotten about the dead men because even a low hood must sleep at nights.

Ed Kibe thought there was no chance of rubbing out this Johnny lug and the girl in the street. He had orders, received on the phone, to watch the pair and tail them until something jelled. Then he had to phone Nat again.

Johnny and Dulcie walked along feeling that life was pretty nice if you were young and healthy. Johnny thought it kind of exciting to have this blonde walking beside him.

They went into a department store, and when they emerged Dulcie was wearing pearl-drop earrings. They hadn't cost the earth, and Johnny had got a kick out of buying them. She was smiling with gleaming eyes and a show of little white teeth.

They started to cross the street. Johnny glanced quickly at the traffic.

Ed Kibe wasn't so quick that moment or maybe he had gotten tired of being a shadow. Anyway, Johnny saw him.

'Ed Kibe!' he thought. 'Now that's strange! How long has this been going on?'

He escorted Dulcie over the road, quickening the pace, and turned her into a store doorway, looked at some display mirrors and waited.

'Don't look around now, baby!' he muttered, 'but there's a guy called Ed Kibe following us.'

Dulcie stared into the store window. 'That heel!'

'Looks like Nat knows we're back in town.'

They got into Dulcie's cream convertible and drove to the motel.

11

Johnny was a bit argumentative. 'It's like this. You've heard of cops and robbers. You know, the films, the TV drammers! So they go together like strawberries and cream, hamburgers and beer. I'm not a cop. You're not a cop. I never robbed anyone — so far as I can remember, anyway. And you — '

'That's where you and I differ,' Dulcie said. 'I used to rob people with Nat in the old days. I'm bad, remember?'

'Phooey,' Johnny said. 'You don't have to be bad. And you've finished with prison. You're paid up. You said you were as good as anyone else remember.'

Dulcie gave him a soft smile. 'Boy, you make me feel nice. But it's like ice cream. It won't last.'

'Aw, let's get dressed. I need a smoke, anyway. Look, what do we do about Nat? Can we just forget a thing like this?'

'I guess I hate him,' she said softly. 'But

maybe I'll have to get him out of my mind.'

'So we just talk about it like that! A rotten crime like takin' another man's life! Wrap it up with a few words! Look, baby. I don't see why that guy should get away with it!'

Johnny was still feeling that way when they were dressed. He took the gun from his pocket and left it in his cabin. It was too heavy for the rayon jacket.

They strolled away from the motel and leaned against a wood rail fencing a children's playing field.

'Was there any kids between you and Doris?' Dulcie asked.

'No!' He was abrupt. 'She thought — well, they wouldn't have fitted.'

'I like kids,' said Dulcie softly.

'You?' Corners of his eyes crinkled as he stared.

'Why not me?' she asked defiantly.

'Why not?' he said slowly. 'Could be you'd make a healthy mother. I wonder who'll be the father?'

A man called Gentleman Ted spotted them at that moment and strolled along.

He had a cigarette between firm, pleasant lips, which, however, could snarl when he changed from a gent to a Nat Franz hood. Right now he was acting nice. He was pleasingly arrayed in a fawn light-weight suit.

He knew exactly who to look for, and he knew he would find them at the motel. Nat's hustlers had located Dulcie and Johnny. Nat had hired a man called Shamus Tracy, who had been a private richard until the police took away his licence. Shamus Tracy knew all the quick routines for finding people and he used a phoney detective licence to get results.

Gentleman Ted walked up to Dulcie, leaned on the rail and smiled at her.

'Dulcie Grande! Of all people! I knew it. How are ya, Dulcie? Don't ya remember me — Ted Klein?'

She stared. 'Should I?'

'Yep.' He looked hurt. 'I knew ya in Los Angeles. You were in cahoots with that slob Nat Franz. I remember he sent ya to the pen.'

'I don't remember you.' She looked interested.

'Well, sugar, I remember you. Sure, we never got around to talkin', but I remember seeing ya at the joints in L.A. You were with that chiseller Nat Franz. Say, don't ya know that guy's right here in Las Vegas?'

'I know that.'

'Yeah, an' that is the guy who got you a rap! I was mighty sore about it at the time. I'd have given that guy, Franz, a workin' for free.' Gentleman Ted glanced at Johnny Lebaron. 'You two got a racket here in L.V.?'

Dulcie laughed. 'You got things wrong, Mister Klein. This is Johnny Lebaron, and he's strictly a straight guy.'

Gentleman Ted grinned at Johnny. 'Hiyah. Forget anythin' I said, will ya? Me — I guess I talk too much!'

'Dulcie has given me her life story,' joked Johnny. 'That's all over now. She's not going back to crime.'

Gentleman Ted looked surprised. He acted it nicely, too. Putting on an act was part of his many abilities.

'Well, ya might think it screwy, but I think ya're doin' the right thing. Me, I'm a crazy guy. I never learn.'

Ted Klein had them laughing and unsuspecting. Dulcie thought maybe the guy had seen her in L.A. Maybe he had known about her, although she knew nothing about him.

She didn't realise that Nat Franz had divulged one or two little facts to Gentleman Ted. They were not very important facts and would certainly never harm one Nat Franz, but Ted Klein had learnt that Dulcie was a gal whom Nat had worked with in Los Angeles and that she had been in the pen through his machinations and she was now a pain in the neck and he wanted to do her bad. The last bit went for Johnny Lebaron, too.

'Say, Dulcie, that bit in the pen don't seem to have harmed ya. You look mighty sweet. Or am I sayin' the wrong things in front of the wrong guy.'

'He's a right guy!'

'That's what I figured. Say, let's have a drink. Gee, I run through the lettuce like it didn't matter. You couldn't lend me fifty bucks, could ya?'

'Mister Klein, I'm a working gal.'

'The brush off!' He sighed. 'Say, let's have that drink.'

They had the drink in the motel barroom. It was nice and it was iced and Gentleman Ted paid. As he had reached out to carry the glasses he held two tiny tablets between finger and thumb. He dropped the tablets into the glasses, spread his fingers and picked up the glasses all in a few seconds. There was no room for uncertainty. He brought two glasses over to Johnny and Dulcie and then went back to the bar for his own drink. He made sure there was no chance of the drinks being mixed!

Gentleman Ted had to get busy on his next act pretty quickly. 'Say, show me your cabins, will ya? I might stick around here if I like the joint and figure to meet up with some suckers.'

'Can we recommend you to the proprietor?' asked Johnny ironically.

Gentleman Ted roared with laughter. Somehow he got them to drink off quickly and walk along to the chalets. Less than a minute later, Dulcie was showing Ted Klein the cute folding bed, the luxury fittings and the rest of the setup.

'Seems okay,' said the crook. 'Maybe I'll book in. Maybe I'll have me a looksee for some mugs. Right now I'm interested in these dames who haveta stick around Las Vegas for six weeks to get a divorce. You'd be surprised most of these judies have dough an' they part with it to a guy like me. Now I know you don't like the sound of that, Mister Lebaron, but ya got to excuse me. I'm like what the judge said — a menace to society but I don't do any real harm — I — '

Gentleman Ted knew he had to keep talking. Those pellets would take effect quickly.

As he talked, Dulcie sat down on a chair and leaned back with a puzzled expression. Some moments later, Johnny glanced down at her. He didn't understand why she looked so tired. He couldn't think so well.

Johnny groped for a chair and sat close to the girl. He stared at her; put out a hand slowly and tried to shake her. She just held her breath stupidly. He didn't seem able to shake her very well. A weary feeling was tightening like a band in his head.

Some moments later he glanced up at Gentleman Ted Klein and caught the savage grin on his face.

Johnny lurched. 'You — you — '

Ted Klein pushed him down again. 'Siddown, sucker. Get to sleep. You think I got nothin' better to do than yap?'

Johnny could not muster the strength to resist. A wave of sleepiness made him slump in the chair. He lolled and nearly fell to the ground. Ted Klein caught him, and prevented any loud noises, then went to the cabin door and locked it. After that he gave his energies to lowering Johnny and the girl to the floor.

'You two suckers will be like that a long time. But I don't want anyone lookin' in here.' He went to the windows and quickly drew the blinds. Then, retreating to the door, he turned the key and went out.

He did not go far. He drove out along the highway and braked his auto close to a big black sedan. The driver of the sedan was none other than Nat Franz, and he had been patiently waiting.

Gentleman Ted left his car and got into the sedan. 'Okay. You can roll this heap into the motel. That joint is easy. It's an easy come, easy go dump. No one will ask questions.'

'Have you fixed them the way you figured?'

'Sure. Just the way I planned. It's a trick. You gotta know how to handle people.'

Nat started the motor. 'Fine. I can give ya a bonus for this, Ted.'

'Don't strain your half-dozen bank accounts!' sneered Gentleman Ted. 'I wonder why you really want those two.'

'I told ya. They did me dirt.'

'Yeah, but how?'

Nat rolled the auto along the highway. 'You don't want to know too much, Gent. What's it to you? Just take the dough an' forget it.'

Ted was silent, smoking a yellow cigarette. Then: 'Seems like to me you figure to rub them out. I'm not in on that.

I don't like homicide. An' your dough ain't worth it.'

Nat Franz leaned his big body against the seat leather, and thinking of Ed Kibe, said: 'Don't worry about anything. Tell you what I'll do. I'll double your money. All ya have to do is scram and shut up. After we get them into this sedan.'

Gentleman Ted nodded and thought, what the hell! Working for Nat was never a whole time job!

They drove into the motel some time later, but instead of taking the sedan into the parking lot, drew up at the cabin door.

Gentleman Ted unlocked the door, allowed Nat Franz to squeeze into the cabin. Then the door was closed but not locked; Ted Klein kept his back to it.

Getting Johnny and Dulcie into the black sedan required some patience and skill. First, the door of the car was left swinging open. Then, when a look-around revealed no one on the site, Johnny Lebaron was walked out to the car, and Dulcie a moment later.

Gentleman Ted and Nat Franz managed the whole thing without any trouble.

The hot afternoon had driven a lot of residents indoors. Others were in the bar or at the pool. If any noticed the scene from cabin windows, they saw nothing startling in it. Drunks at motels were common enough.

A minute later, with the sedan rolling out of the motel, Nat Franz relaxed. He thought things were going his way at last. He had had some bad times with these two, but the play was drawing to a close.

The sedan sliced along the highway, in the direction of Las Vegas. Gentleman Ted got out of the auto when his own car was reached. Nat Franz handed him a wad of bills that he had no need to count because he knew to a buck the exact amount.

'Thanks, Ted. Just start forgettin'.'

'I've never seen these suckers before.' Ted Klein flashed a glance at Dulcie's slim body reclining naturally in a corner of the rear seating. 'But I sure took a fancy to that babe!' He got into his auto and drove off very fast.

Nat Franz went along at a reasonable speed, feeling there was no hurry. The knockout tablets should keep these two quiet for hours. That gave him all the time he wanted.

A dope would have turned around and pumped lead into the two unconscious persons. Or even used a knife to bring death. Nat wanted none of these methods. He wasn't even going to do the job himself. All he wanted was the knowledge that they were out of the way.

He did not have to drive into town. His destination was on the outskirts of Las Vegas. That was all to the good because he did not have to stop at traffic lights and risk someone noticing his passengers.

He finally drove into a scrap yard that ran along some railroad sidings. He stopped the auto amid the piles and waited for the man who'd help him dispose of two bodies.

12

Johnny Lebaron stirred drowsily. He took about ten minutes to really come round. It was an awakening from sodden sleep. His first thought was that he had a terrible hangover. Then he thought that was queer because he wasn't a guy for a lot of booze. He pushed himself up into a sitting position. His head felt swimmy. His tongue tasted like bitter dregs.

Memories returned slowly. Thoughts of Gentleman Ted and the chalet flashed into his mind. Johnny glanced sideways and found Dulcie lying beside him.

The surroundings worried him. They were lying in a big steel tank about ten feet square. If first impressions were of any value, they were trapped. Nat Franz had struck again! Ted Klein was a stooge. Hell, there was no need to go into that any further! Nat had located them at the motel and got them. That was all! He didn't want a blueprint as to how and why.

Johnny bent over Dulcie and tried to accelerate the awakening process. He shook her gently and she opened her eyes. She stared at him and smiled. Then the smile faded into a frown. He thought she could look fascinating even when she frowned, and that this was a crazy time to get such ideas!

'Waken up, baby. We're in another jam.'

Eventually, she got to her feet and, with a little assistance, walked around the tank. Pretty swiftly, the danger dawned on her.

'It's a trap! We can't get out, Johnny!'

He nodded grimly.

'Yep. Pally Nat Franz never lets up evidently. Where the hell we are I don't know! All we can see is the sky and these damned metal walls. Isn't a break anywhere, and they're about fifteen feet high, I guess.'

'Can we climb out?'

'How, baby? Can you climb smooth walls? Okay, let's try something. You get on my shoulders. Stand on them. See how far you can reach. Let's go. You feel steady enough?'

'I'd feel better if I had a cup of coffee,' she admitted.

'A cup of java! Ring for service, baby. On second thoughts don't even think about ringing anythin'. I've a hunch pally Franz is drumming up something unpleasant. We're not in this tank for nothing.'

She climbed onto his shoulders, and raised herself to a standing position, while Johnny steadied her ankles.

'How far can you reach, baby?'

Dulcie stretched her hands heavenwards. 'The top is about three feet away! I can't reach it, Johnny! I just can't!'

'Take it easy,' he growled. 'Now for some gymnastics, sugar. I'm going to lift you with my hands under your shoes. That ought to give you another few feet. Don't wobble when I lift. Look up. And remember you can always fall on me.'

The stunt was not so easy. He managed to elevate her and she did her part by keeping steady and leaning against the smooth tank wall. In spite of these efforts, her fingertips were inches from the rim of the tank.

She clawed at the red rust as if there

was some magical way of hauling herself up. She broke her fingernails and scraped rust down into Johnny's face. He tightened his eyes and shook the stream of grit from his face, holding her as high as possible. Her weight was no great trouble. It was maddening to think that the rim of the tank was only inches from her fingers.

'Look, baby,' he jerked. 'There's only one way. I'm going to throw you up! Maybe I can heave you up. Try to grab hold of the tank rim. If you get a grip, haul yourself up. How the hell you'll get down the other side I don't know. But if you can, beat it — get help — anything!'

'I can't leave you, Johnny!'

'Quit that kind of screwy talk! Get out of this tank and you can get help. Unless you want to try throwin' me up!'

'Okay, Johnny, I'm ready,' she said grimly.

She waited with outstretched hands, confident that if she failed Johnny would catch her as she fell. He inspired confidence. He was a right guy. Maybe her right guy except that he was married.

That was another screwy thought to have in such a precarious situation.

'Ready?' grated Johnny.

'Sure.'

He whipped her up as if he was throwing a tree trunk into the air. Dulcie grabbed at the tank rim and hung on grimly.

She tried to pull herself up by digging her knees against the rusty wall and attempted to get some purchase that way. She increased her hold on the rim; got an arm over. Then she heaved herself up with savage determination. She balanced precariously on the narrow rim, her body resting on it and her legs dangling in space.

She immediately encountered something that nearly shocked her off her perch.

There was a ladder placed against the outside wall of the tank, and in the act of ascending the ladder was a man. She had never seen the man before. She realised, however, that his intentions were homicidal.

The man was hauling up a hosepipe.

He had the end coiled around his shoulder. The pipe trailed away across the scrap yard. Dulcie got the idea at once. It looked like this man intended to pour water into the tank so that they should drown like rats!

The man halted when he saw the girl haul herself to the tank rim. His little wrinkled face stared up. Dulcie watched him in fear. Then her scare passed and was replaced by a terrific rage. She moved along the tank rim until she got to the top of the ladder.

By that time the little man had dropped the pipe. He went down the ladder and picked up a length of metal rod that was lying beside a pile of junk. Then he began to climb again.

Dulcie called down to Johnny. 'There's a guy on a ladder and he's coming up. He was aiming to fix up a hosepipe to his tank. Guess the idea was to drown us like rats in a sewer. Nice, don't you think?'

Johnny Lebaron instinctively placed hands to the rusting tank wall, wishing he could leap like Superman. He groaned helplessly. There just wasn't anything he could do to help the girl perched so coolly on the tank rim.

'Watch him, Dulcie!' he shouted. 'Ain't there anyone around you can shout to?'

'Can't see anyone,' she answered. 'This is a junkyard. Full of old scrap, mostly metal. Doesn't seem to be anyone else around. The place is very quiet.'

'Trust Nat to pick the right spot.'

He strode around the tank. There was not a bolt head or an angle-iron. He examined the welded seams, saw they were smooth. There wasn't a valve or an inspection manhole. He had no idea of the original purpose of the tank. Probably it had had an industrial use and was now scrap. It was solid enough. He tried kicking the walls. All he got was a dull hollow noise.

Then he stared desperately at Dulcie. She was sitting at the top of the ladder, waiting.

The ugly little man ascended the ladder slowly, pausing on every rung. There was no mistaking his intention. He gripped the metal rod menacingly . . .

Dulcie stared in fascination. The man's

119

numerous halts built up an unbearable tension. She wondered how she could cope with a man armed with a chunk of steel. Probably he figured to brain her so that she would drop back into the tank. Even if Johnny broke her fall, she would be half dead. And if the man got the hosepipe up and turned on the water, the end would be lousy.

The man came up another step, grinning coarsely. Dulcie wondered about the setup. Had Nat Franz left the method of their death to this murderous little runt? It seemed that way, for they could have been killed while in their drugged sleep.

The man ascended another rung. He was only a couple of yards below her now. It occurred to her that she could push the ladder outwards; but she realised that it could be the means of escape for Johnny if she got rid of this horrible, crawling runt.

The man moved up a bit more. He halted, leered at her. Dulcie stared, nursing a sullen anger. She knew now why people killed. She wanted to kill this creature. He stood in the way of escape. More than that, he represented a brutal death for Johnny and herself.

Suddenly the man leapt another rung and swung the rod. Dulcie slid to one side with a jerk. The rod clanged on the tank rim.

The man laughed softly as if with enjoyment. He had the rod ready for another blow. It came, slashing the air, aiming at Dulcie's head.

She tried to avoid the striking metal by swaying to one side. She was sitting on the tank rim, her legs on the top run of the ladder, her hands raised for protection.

The rod missed her as she swayed, but struck her on the shoulder. Pain flooded violently through her. She tried to claw at the rod, but it whipped out of her reach.

The animalistic man leered triumphantly and swung the rod again. Dulcie did not move. Instead, she clawed frantically at the descending weapon. A crazy prayer ripped through her mind. With her desperate, sobbing attempt to fight back came the answering miracle. The rod slammed into her cupped hands.

She did not feel any pain. The blow could have broken her wrist. It did not. Instead, she gripped savagely at the rod, and pulled hard. Like lightning, she reversed her tactics and pushed the rod back. The jab caught the little man by surprise. He teetered on the ladder and had to whip out a hand to steady himself.

Dulcie had no coherent idea of what she was doing. She was simply fighting for survival and drawing strength from some unknown source. As the murderous man took one hand from the length of rod, she tugged with all her strength. The rod scraped out of the man's grasp. He balanced, tried to whip up a hand to grab the rod again. Then Dulcie struck at him.

The blow was only one of many. She rained them furiously. The man swayed on the ladder like some horrible drunken figure, then, suddenly, dived to one side and hit the earth.

Johnny had seen only a part of the struggle, and had suffered agony. He'd been up there with Dulcie, urging her on, fighting invisibly with her. Sweat gleamed on his face. His pupils were dilated. His hands were knotted balls of murder.

He sensed it was all over. He didn't have to be told anything. He saw her droop.

'Hang on, Dulcie! Just sit tight, baby! Take it easy. It's all over, isn't it?'

She nodded. A minute later she had recovered from the reaction. 'I'll heave this ladder up and work it down to you. After you get up here, you can do the graft.'

The ladder proved heavy, but she managed to lower it to Johnny. He went up it swifter than a house-painter after a bonus. At the top, he held Dulcie; and she held onto him. It was like that for a moment. Then he got the ladder propped on the outside of the tank, and helped her down. Soon they were looking at the sprawled, unmoving man, the ladder and the death tank.

Johnny dropped to one knee and made a swift examination of the fallen man.

'He's dead,' he said briefly. His eyes strayed to the bloodied metal rod lying near the body, where Dulcie had dropped it when handling the ladder. Dulcie

123

followed his gaze, became distraught as the implications of what had happened sank in.

'Hell, Johnny!' she gasped. 'My prints will be all over that rod! And the police have my fingerprints on file! They'll get me for murder! I've got to wipe that rod — '

Johnny grabbed her as she tried to pick up the rod.

'Relax, baby! Just leave it. It's pointless you doing that. Your fingerprints are all over the inside of that tank, and along the top — we don't know exactly where. It'd take us hours and hours to wipe them all clean. But you don't have to worry about the cops finding that guy's body anyway.'

'What do you mean?'

'That dead guy was working for Nat. You can bet he'll be along here soon, to handle the disposal of our bodies. When he finds that body instead, you can be sure he'll dispose of it where the cops can't find it. The last thing Nat wants is the cops investigating a suspicious death.'

'Why not?' Dulcie was still anxious and unconvinced.

'Because they might easily find things that link him to Nat. Payments to his bank account, maybe. You see what I mean?'

Dulcie nodded. 'I guess so. But what do we do now?'

'We scram out of here as quickly as possible before Nat — or more likely one of his strong-arm boys — shows up. Let's get going!'

As they went, Johnny muttered: 'Maybe I ought to kill Nat Franz!'

13

Johnny had not been robbed during the events with Gentleman Ted or Nat Franz, and was able to pay for a cab, which took them swiftly to the motel.

They cleaned up, Dulcie using a new dress and all that went with it. Even her shoes had been spoilt when she had scraped them against the rusty tank. She was sheathed in an alluring blue dress when next Johnny Lebaron saw her. He thought that blonde hair and blue went well together, and wondered if he was in love with her.

They needed a drink badly. So they went to the bedroom and set them up. Dulcie drank two martinis, and Johnny two rye whiskies and a chaser of beer.

Suddenly Dulcie said: 'You're not thinking of really killing Nat Franze, are you?'

He was surprised. 'Did I say that? I've forgotten. Anyway, I've no right to kill anyone. It's the law's job to send Nat to perdition.'

'If you'd been killed,' she said in a low voice, 'I'd have gone gunning for Nat Franz.'

'Baby, it couldn't have happened like that. We were set up to be killed together. Because we know too much. That's all.'

'What if I'd been killed?' Dulcie watched his expression intently.

He lowered his glass. 'I'd be tempted to kill the guy with my two hands!'

She leaned back, smiled quietly and smoked. He watched her curiously, noting the way the smoke dribbled from her soft red lips. He sensed she had something on her mind and he wondered what it was.

'Let's get out of this motel,' Johnny urged. 'I don't feel safe. Hell, if I had only one bit of documentary evidence, I'd go talk to the police.'

'Never mind the cops,' Dulcie remarked. 'I don't like 'em. You can guess why.'

They checked out of the motel after the drinks. 'Look, where do we live?' Johnny asked, as he tooled the convertible along the road. 'Do we stick another night in

Las Vegas? If we do and go into an hotel, we might find Nat's hoodlums on our tails in no time.'

'We'll stick in Las Vegas as long as we want,' Dulcie snapped. She was thinking that Nat Franz shouldn't be allowed to live more than another night.

Eventually they moved into a rooming house on Alamo Avenue. They got two rooms and paid for them in advance. The old turkey who handed them the keys looked hard at Johnny Lebaron. Dulcie got searching glances, but she handed some back. The old turkey departed and thought that dough was the only thing that made sense.

There was a garage in an alley at the back where Johnny parked Dulcie's car. He went to her room and they sat and talked. Later he kissed her. Again it was an electric thing that started with calculated coolness and went on to a burning fusion of lips, impulses, yearnings. Talk was out then. He didn't say he loved her. She, too, kept secrets and used her lips for the kiss.

She said softly: 'Wipe your lips, Johnny.

The old dame will notice.'

'Did you ever think of getting' married?'

'Sure. All gals think of getting married.'

'Yeah.' He put the handkerchief away; looked sideways. 'Was there ever a guy? Did you ever have a steady?'

'Yeah, sure. Long ago.' She paused. 'Before I met all the wrong guys.'

'Well, what happened to him?'

'I don't know. He just went away, somehow. I forgot him. So what? You want my past?'

'No.' He fumbled for his cigarette case. 'Like hell I do! Just stay the way you are — Dulcie Grande, the gal who picked me up. The gal who walked in on me. That's the only Dulcie I want to know.'

'Okay, you know me. Do I know you? You're married — sure. You're an engineer. You know all about metallurgy and spans and stresses. You've kissed me: saved my life; I'm happy with you. But nothing has added up yet.'

'What d'you mean?'

'We don't know where we're going. That's what I mean.'

He shifted uneasily. 'Baby, a helluva lot of people are just the same and they get into a wooden jacket at the end and still don't know the answers.'

'I was thinking of your Doris!' she snapped, and stubbed an inch long cigarette end.

He swung his head; avoided her eyes. 'She might divorce me,' he muttered.

It was about the last significant word. She switched on a radio, and they listened and smoked. There wasn't any TV. The rooming house didn't run to that.

Because it was stuffy in the house, he had taken off his jacket. She noted the bulge of the gun. They went out later and had some tea in a small café nearby. They watched other people warily. Johnny began to think that all sorts of people could look like potential thugs.

On returning to the rooms, he became somewhat moody at the inactive role he was forced into. He realized Nat Franz was governing his actions. He didn't know what to do. All he could think of were the chances of tipping off the police.

Dulcie Grande had more decided

ideas, but she had no intention of telling Johnny Lebaron anything.

She stalled along until night arrived. The night was better for grim decisions. She finally moved when she was able to take the gun out of Johnny's pocket without his knowledge.

'I'm going to my room,' she said. 'I might rest.'

He nodded and she went out. She moved quickly through her room and picked up a lightweight coat and slipped it on. After that came a crazy hat and a white handbag. She thought it was looking like it had been knocked around, but so what! It was good enough to hold a gun!

Two minutes after leaving Johnny, she went down the stairs silently. She moved through the lobby and went out into the street. She went around to the garage and got the auto rolling.

It was a fine night to kill a swine. This much added up: someone had to stop Nat Franz. Apart from stopping him, she hated him. The guy had gotten away with too much. If they stuck around Las Vegas any more, he might locate them again and try to kill them. She thought she would stop that.

Obviously Nat Franz would be at his headquarters, the Imperial Casino. That was where he lived. Even rats had homes. There wasn't anything unusual in a guy like Franz going home.

She might see him there, but she didn't know how she could kill the man. She had no plan. All she had was a desire to kill.

She had no one to tell herself she was acting upon a homicidal impulse that had taken others to the electric chair and the gas chambers. Plenty of folks had travelled the road, and plenty more would do it in future because people are fools.

When she reached the Imperial Casino, with its façade of light and dark parking lot, she was surprised to see a man getting into a dark sedan. She thought there was something familiar about both. Then it hit her. This was no other than Nat Franz, setting out for someplace.

Surprised, she watched. She had her auto at the curb. There just wasn't time to take her gun out, let alone steel her nerve for the act of drawing a bead. The next moment Nat Franz had the sedan rolling onto the highway.

She had the sense to engage gear and get moving. Within seconds she was trailing the other auto. In this manner they went down the wide streets, turned at two intersections without having to stop for lights. Dulcie was able to keep behind Nat's car easily, although twice another auto had got between them.

The drive went on about a mile, she estimated, and they reached the fringe of the town. She was alert all the time, and when Nat Franz stopped his auto she halted quickly, in the shadows between street lamps.

Nat Franz got out of his car and stood for a moment looking at the glaring entrance to a carnival ground. In the light of hundreds of bulbs, built in an arch, he was visible to Dulcie Grande as a tallish, bulky figure in a dark, conservative suiting.

She stared at the lighted archway, and read in green neon: BIG JACK'S & BIG

RIDES. COME IN AND HAVE FUN.

The sound of amplified records surged on the night air. A number of teenagers were entering the place. Some flashy punks stood at the entrance arch. Dulcie thought it was probably a pickup paradise.

Suddenly Nat Franz went through the lighted arch and disappeared. Dulcie got out of her auto, slammed the door. The fairground was full of youngish folks. The usual roar and rattle wafted all over the place. As she walked on, more slowly, she looked for Nat Franz and wondered what had possessed him to come here.

The noise assailed her from all sides, a mixture of blaring music and grating wheels. On her right a cargo of kids were being hurled around a Martian Maze. A carny at a sideshow was demanding new customers for a strip-tease. She was jostled by groups of people. Some punks eyed her, and there was nothing original in their thoughts. She walked on, and then suddenly spotted Nat Franz again.

The man's big build looked out of

place among the slim punks who crowded up to get into a Tunnel of Love. He was standing beside the ride, staring at the cars as they reappeared from the tunnel.

Dulcie wondered if the man had gone nuts. Maybe killers did go nuts eventually. Then she dismissed the thought. Nat had run his pay-up-or-die racket in a cool, calculated manner. The man was normal. What, then, was he doing on this carny ground?

She didn't think he wanted a ride in a Tunnel of Love. That was too corny. She had a feeling he was looking for someone.

Dulcie stood close to a wood wall that railed off a noisy ride and watched him. She thought she could get a chance to kill him in this sound-filled ground. She would like to know what he was doing here, though.

As she stood, alone, a young punk slouched up and grinned at her. 'You alone, sugar? Wanna try a ride around?'

He was chewing gum; he had a hand-painted necktie; a red hat; a sallow face with a little moustache; a yellow shirt; a cheap suit, colourful enough for the Russian ballet.

'Get moving,' she hissed.

He grinned, took her arm. 'Aw, sweetie, ya don't wanna — '

She whipped the gun from her handbag and jabbed his thin ribs. The man nearly choked. His hand fell from her arm. He walked away, giving her some scared, backward glances.

Dulcie swallowed her anger. She put the gun back into her handbag and looked across the ground for Nat Franz. She couldn't see him. It seemed he had moved away while she was busy with the punk.

She swore, and stepped away from the wall. She thought she would find Nat Franz again somewhere in the carny ground, and when she did she would use the gun.

She walked on, scanning the shows, the rides and alleys between the structures. Then all at once she found him standing in a dark alley between two towering wood walls that supported big rides. There were shadows in the alley.

He was half-turned to Dulcie's view,

talking intently with someone. She just could not make out the other man's appearance. She raised the gun and triggered grimly. She saw Nat Franz stagger in agony. Then she ran like mad.

14

She got clear of the carny ground. The crack of her gun had gone unnoticed in the general noise. She did not wait to see the results of her shot, but got to her auto and drove away very fast.

She was wide-eyed and excited. She was sure she had killed Nat Franz. She had shot at him, seen him stagger. Surely the slug had taken him to his death!

She hardly knew where she was driving, but pretty soon she was back in Alamo Avenue. She decided she would have to tell Johnny what she had done. She thought she had done something great.

After she had garaged the auto, she found Johnny waiting for her in her room. He grabbed at her as she came in and shook her angrily.

'What have you been doing? What's that look on your face?'

'I've killed Nat Franz!'

'It's impossible! Where've you been?'

He grabbed her again. 'Come on, give!'

'Let go of me, you ape!' Dulcie said angrily. 'I don't know why I bothered to come back.'

'Tell me what you've been up to,' he growled.

'I think I've killed Nat!'

'You said that before. What d'you mean — you think?'

'I took your gun — my gun — and shot him. In a carny ground. I saw him fall. Then I ran.'

'How'd you get to the carny ground?'

'I went into the Imperial Casino. Nat was leaving. I figured to kill him, but I couldn't do it right away. He drove to this carny ground, and I followed. When I shot at him he was talking to another guy.'

'What other guy?'

'I didn't really see the feller. So I don't know who he was. Probably some hustler Nat wanted.'

Johnny let go her arms, drew in a deep breath. He snatched the handbag from her and extracted the gun. He smelled the barrel.

'You crazy little bitch! You know what you've done? It's murder!'

'That guy would have got us! He'd know we weren't dead in that tank.'

'Murder!' grated Johnny. 'You're not the law. If you kill another person, it's murder.'

'What about Billy Death? You helped to kill him, didn't you?'

'Fool talk!' He shoved the gun into his jacket pocket. 'That was an accident. The shaft caved in.'

'You took the guy up there!'

'It was still an accident!' he barked. 'I didn't want the guy dead. I'd prefer to hand him over to the cops.'

'Well, I killed that ugly little guy in the junkyard!' she flared tauntingly. 'And if I hadn't you'd be a nasty cadaver by now!'

'You were fighting for your life,' he breathed. 'You have a right to defend yourself. No one has a right to kill another guy — unless it's a war, and even then people are presumed to be defending themselves.'

'Okay, wrap it up.' She was still defiant. 'You'll sure get plenty mixed. Me — I think Nat is dead. I feel good about it.'

'You think! Are you sure? What happened?'

'He staggered. I just ran.'

Johnny bunched one fist into the palm of his other hand.

'If the cops get onto this, what d'you think will happen to you?'

'I don't want to think about that. I think we ought to get out of Las Vegas now.'

Johnny rounded on her again. 'You've got plenty of pep, but no brains! I'm going to check on Nat Franz. Find out what has happened to him. You'll stick here.'

'I don't want to stick in this crummy joint. I'll come with you.'

'You'll stick!' He grabbed her hands and hurt her. 'Get it? You stick. Do as I tell you. I'm goin' along to this carny ground to make inquiries. I'll soon find out if there's been a murder. Even carnies don't like killings on their grounds.'

He was hurting her wrists. 'Johnny, don't fight with me!' she suddenly pleaded.

'All right.' He eased the pressure on her hands. 'Tell me where I find this carny ground. Get this fixed: I'm going over to check, and you're stayin' here.'

'Oh, okay. The ground is over on the eastside of the town. It's called BIG JACK'S & BIG RIDES. I guess you'll find it. Sure, check, Johnny. I guess I'd like to know after all.'

He picked up his hat. 'Keys in the auto?'

'Yeah. I left them in.'

'You stick here. Lock the door and don't answer any knocks,' he warned.

He went out on that, and got the car out of the garage. There was gas; the engine was warm, and he had no trouble in finding the carny ground. In the first place, he got over to the east side very quickly, and then he asked a young guy for instructions. The man was going to the carny ground. Johnny took him along and they arrived minutes later.

Johnny walked into the place, giving scant attention to the giggling teenage girls who eyed his big figure as if he was Tarzan and Superman rolled into one. He walked to the centre of the ground; saw nothing unusual. He stopped near a carny who was re-tracking a cable from a diesel generator.

'Hey, been an accident around here?'

The man looked up. 'Accident? Not that I know of.'

'I'm a private detective. I was told a guy got hurt.'

'I ain't heard about it.'

'I was told it was a murder.'

The carny jerked. 'Hell! Ya crazy! Ya bin told wrong. I've bin around here all night. I ain't heard anythin' about a murder.'

'A guy was shot.' persisted Johnny grimly.

'Say, lissen, ya got the wrong joint. We don't have murders around here. What d'ya think this is anyway? This is a respectable place. Gee, if Big Jack could hear ya he'd be plenty mad.'

'Sure there wasn't any shooting?' Johnny made a last effort.

'The only shootin' is over by the galleries!' snarled the man. 'Get goin'. Maybe you ain't a dick. I heard that spiel before. I've a good mind to — '

Johnny Lebaron walked until he was a good way from the man. He stopped near a ride called the Tunnel of Love, lit a cigarette and watched the procession of cars rattle into the tunnel.

He began to grin. The grin became a chuckle and then a deep-throated laugh. 'You're some killer, baby!' he muttered. 'I'm mighty glad you missed that guy.'

As he grinned something hissed past his ear and dully into a board at his side.

He alerted in a split second. His grin flashed away, and a thousand warnings tingled through his brain. Instinctively he stepped lithely to one side.

At the same time he heard the curious, fierce hiss and the sound of a small, hard object digging into wood again.

The answer shrieked at him. He was being shot at by a silenced gun.

He thrust swiftly into a crowd of people. The man shooting wouldn't want to hit the wrong person. He had had two misses already, the first by an inch and the second because Johnny had moved quickly.

The silenced gat prompted grim

thoughts of the adhesive tape bindings lying on the floor of the shanty at the old silver mine. He had wondered how Nat had gotten out of the bindings. Now he knew.

Johnny did not stand more than two seconds in any one place. He thought the best insurance policy was to keep moving, but fast! He shot swift glances all around as he weaved through groups of people, and presently spotted a man walking steadily through the carny ground. The man had his arms folded. Johnny knew he was hiding a gun under his armpit. It was a cute trick; all you had to do was turn sideways to aim; That was tricky marksmanship and probably accounted for the man missing the first time.

Johnny watched Billy Death walk steadily towards the entrance arch. He looked normal, a teenage punk in baggy trousers and cheap silk shirt and tousled hair.

Johnny suddenly knew why Nat Franz had visited the carny ground. He trotted back to Dulcie's auto and got into the seat. Yeah, Nat had gone to the carny ground for a good reason. Because Billy Death was there. That was it. Apparently Nat Franz wanted his strange gunny. Sure. Nat knew the death tank gimmick had failed. It wasn't hard to guess who was scheduled to be rubbed out.

15

Johnny Lebaron held Dulcie in his arms. The way he was kissing her, he was just a big brother comforting her. They'd just finished throwing some angry words. She had wanted to go out shooting for Nat Franz again, and he had stopped her. She had been angry. They were all mixed up. They ended in each other's arms. It was as crazy as that.

'Look, baby, you must have missed Nat with that shot.'

'I saw the guy stagger!'

'Well, okay, you pipped him. But it couldn't have been too bad. If we could locate him now, we'd probably find him having attention for a flesh wound.'

'I hope it hurts the swine!'

'It'll hurt, but he'll get over it. There was a good reason for him being at the carny ground. He was seeing Billy Death. That was probably the guy he was talking to.'

'But — Billy — Death — gee — '

'Yeah. He wasn't killed in the shaft. He got Nat out of his bindings. Guess Billy found another exit to the shaft. Can only be that. Nat has put Billy Death onto us. What are we going to do about it?'

'Give me a cigarette,' she muttered. 'Aw, gee, you know something, Johnny — I'm getting awful sick of this run-around. I wish I'd killed Nat. Now we're back at the starting tapes. There's one thing — Nat can't know we're living here.'

Johnny Lebaron lit cigarettes. 'He'll try to locate us again. I don't know how he'll do it, but maybe he will. Unless we locate him.'

'What do you mean by that?' Dulcie perched herself on the chair arm.

'Look, baby, we've got to end this thing somehow. I guess it ends one of three ways. We can beat it to another town — make it a thousand miles away. Or we wait for Nat to start a kill feast. Or, maybe, we get him and his stooge and take them to the cops.'

'You missed out a fourth. We could kill

Nat and his stooge.'

'We're not killers,' he snapped. 'That's the last way we'll do it.'

'All right, you're so high and mighty!' she flared. 'Just let Nat come along and blast us into next week!'

'Look, cool down, will you? The way you act you'd think I was your enemy! Let me tell you something, baby. You'd be a beautiful corpse by now if it hadn't been for me!'

'Yeah!' she yelled. 'And you'd be back with your damned Doris!'

They glared for some time. They were getting on each other's nerves. They didn't understand why they were so mixed.

Johnny rose, walked around the room irritably. The way she had taunted him about Doris stuck in his mind. Maybe he was the biggest fool ever. He stabbed at the window drapes; parted them and stared moodily into the street.

He saw the shape of a man waiting on the other side of the road. There was nothing to identify him. Just a figure that moved occasionally in the dark. It was

149

this very attitude that made Johnny Lebaron suspicious. He thought hunted people got suspicious.

He let the drapes fall back into place. 'I'm out of cigarettes. I'll go get some.'

'I'll come with you.'

'You can stay right here. I won't be long.'

She thrust her hands to her hips, adopted a defiant stance. Her blue eyes glinted fury. She looked like something off a magazine cover, with that blue dress curving to her and the electric light gleaming on her blonde hair.

'If all you want is cigarettes, you can take me along! I'm not staying here, I tell you!'

'All right. Stick your coat on — and that nutty hat, if you like! And shaddup!'

They went down the stairs a minute later. In the lobby he told her he had seen a man hanging around in the shadows.

'I'm suspicious. Could be nothing. And it could be one of Nat's hired gunnies. If it is, I don't know how he found us.'

'That guy never lets up!'

'Now play it my way, honey,' he

pleaded. 'Keep quiet and stay behind me.'

'Sure, Johnny, sure.'

He eased to the door, stayed in the shadow long enough to adjust his eyes to the view across the street. He saw the man lurking on the other side. There was something about his manner, something Johnny couldn't explain that clinched his suspicions. Still he wasn't able to identify the man except that he was of medium height and wore dark clothes.

Johnny eased himself through the doorway and went down the steps while Dulcie hung back in the lobby.

The man on the other side of the street saw Johnny. Johnny knew it when a silenced slug whistled past his face. He kept on moving fast. As another peculiar 'plop' sounded and the slug whistled, he dived for a basement well that lay in front of the rooming house window.

Billy Death! How he had gotten to Alamo Avenue was a question to be answered later. He had not wasted any time and it couldn't be anyone else with that silenced gat.

Johnny wondered how the devil he was

going to get out of this one and flashed a glance up to the half-open doorway. Dulcie was behaving. She was still in the lobby. He hoped to heaven she stayed there.

He felt the shape of the .45 in his pocket. If he used it, the row would waken Alamo Avenue. It brought back the old question: was he prepared to kill to get out of the mess? He decided he wasn't. There was another angle, audacious, with Billy holding all the trumps. Maybe he could do it, at that.

The way he figured it, Billy was the guy who could slick the cops on Nat Franz and stop this hell-around. That made sense. The day the cops took over would be pretty good.

Billy Death had to talk himself and his boss right into the gas chamber. It was a heck of an idea to come to a man crouching in a dirty basement well, watching another man in fear of death.

Johnny moved. There was an old-fashioned iron rail fringing the basement areas of all the houses in Alamo Avenue, and stretching down the street on the inside of the sidewalk. Johnny moved out of the well and slid into the next one, using the cover of the thick iron rail.

He had to get away, and then surprise Billy Death. How, he did not know. The queer young guy would be wary.

Johnny slid through another basement area. There was a bad moment when he had to pass a street lamp and he wondered if his slithering movement could be detected. Apparently Billy Death did not realise he was well away from the basement well of the rooming house. Johnny got past the light and then hastened his movements, undulating in and out of the wells, keeping below the level of the rails all the time. He was mighty glad when he reached the bottom of the street and crossed over, walking slowly, like a passing stranger.

He ran up a dark alley and encountered an opening that was constructed between the row of houses, so that there was an archway giving access to the street where Billy Death now waited.

Johnny slowed considerably when he reached the archway. He crept along and halted behind Billy Death. He could see the man standing close to an unlighted street standard. Johnny blessed his crepe soles. He inched a bit further, crouched, and came out of hiding. Too late Billy Death turned his head, suspicion in every movement.

Johnny leaped at him, clawing for the gun he could now see. It was the first thing he gripped. He forced it down and then began a vicious twist to make Billy drop it.

Billy Death was not the guy for a rough house. Johnny wrenched his hand round to breaking point, and the gun dropped. It made more noise clattering to the sidewalk than it ever did in exploding. Then he brought up a bunched fist into Billy's chin. It was a ball of iron-hard knuckles propelled by a sinewy arm, and the result was Billy Death went limp. Johnny gripped him like a sack and hauled him across the road. Dulcie rushed out to assist him.

'I can handle this gink!' grunted Johnny. 'Look, baby, go over the road and find the guy's gun. He dropped it beside that unlit standard.'

There'd be hell to pay if the old rooming-house turkey discovered what was going on. Johnny swung Billy Death across his back in a firefighter's lift and went up the stairs cat-footed.

A minute later he was inside his room. He dumped the man and had to slam him again on the jaw to make him sleep! Then Dulcie came into the room and closed the door, turned the key. She had the gun. Johnny took it, spent a moment examining it curiously.

'Some toy!' he muttered. The gat was valuable, the clincher. He had only a hazy idea of cops' procedure, but he did know something about ballistics. Slugs from this gun would have identical markings. The police ought to have the murder slugs as exhibits. They would know the murders had been committed by the same gun and presumably the same man.

Johnny stared down at Billy Death and smiled grimly.

'What's that look?' asked Dulcie. 'You've got a smile like you'd found a hundred spot bill.'

He told her why he was smiling. She got the idea and laughed excitedly.

'Gee, we've got 'em! We got that lousy so-and-so!'

'Yeah, seems like we got Nat and his homicidal pal.'

Billy Death came out of the mists. He looked sick and his face was unusually white. He blinked up at Johnny Lebaron.

'Let me go! You can't keep me here!'

Johnny narrowed his eyes. The man had a split personality. One side of him was harmless; the other hounded by a strange impulse to stalk and kill. Without a gun, Billy Death was not dangerous.

'We're taking you to the police, Billy. They'll want you for what you've done. Why not talk? Nat Franz hired you to kill men, didn't he?'

'That's my gun!' Billy ignored the questions. He didn't seem to hear them. He seemed worried because his prized gun was out of his possession.

'How'd you get here, Billy? How'd you find us?'

'Followed ya. I had an auto outside the carny ground. I just hung on your tail.'

Johnny nodded encouragingly. 'So you've got an auto somewhere! You saw me on the carny ground, and thought you'd get me right away. You didn't, so you followed up. Nat gave you the word, huh? Nat Franz know we're here?'

Billy lowered his head, sullenly.

'He doesn't, huh?' continued Johnny. 'That's fine. How about Nat? Was he shot?'

Billy Death's sleepy eyes suddenly gleamed as he glanced at Dulcie.

'She shot him! He was wounded in the shoulder. He told me to get you two!'

Johnny rammed the silenced gun into his pocket. 'We've got enough for the cops. They'll wrap it up. Dulcie, go phone the police and get them over here right away. After that it's their job to pick up Nat Franz!'

'Yeah?' Billy Death bounded up in a frenzy.

16

Billy Death was not a rough house slogger, but he had a great deal of litheness. He sprang like a furious animal bent only on escape and was across the room in seconds. Johnny went after him with outstretched hands. With incredible speed, Billy thrust through the window and turned, clinging to a nearby drainpipe. Johnny tried to grab at him. A foot kicked out and caught him in the face. Lights exploded in his head, but he charged back with clearer vision and was in time to see Billy Death sliding down the drainpipe.

Johnny grabbed at his gun, then hesitated. He cursed. He didn't want the man dead. He jumped back: collided with Dulcie. He cursed again, and she got out of his way. He rushed to the door, Dulcie following him, but by the time they reached the street. Billy Death was a speeding figure down the road.

'Goin' for his auto! He'll reach it before

I get near him! I know where he's goin'! Let's get our auto out, Dulcie!'

It was all time and work. They dashed around to the garage where Johnny had stuck the auto after returning from the carny ground. They got in and drove out. There wasn't anyone around to throw questions. There wasn't any chance to leave a message for the police.

He drove out of Alamo Avenue, hit the bright lights. He did not see Billy Death anywhere. He did not know what sort of auto the young guy used, anyway.

Johnny felt sure he knew where Billy Death was going! The young gunny would tear back to Nat Franz.

Johnny knew he could drive to the nearest cop station and hand the mess over to them. The thought was just a mere whisper. He was a man right in there, angry, determined, possessed with an urge to do something about it himself.

In this sombre mood, he drove up to the Imperial Casino, rolling into the parking lot and stopping with a suddenness that tested the auto's independent suspension.

As he got out, with Dulcie at his side, silent and wondering, he knew he hadn't a shred of plan for dealing with Nat Franz or Billy Death. He just had the urge to get hold of them. It did occur to him that it was like gripping a couple of rattle-snakes!

There were autos in the parking lot, but he did not know if one belonged to Billy Death. 'Let's get in there, Dulcie, and see what we can make out of this rumpus. One thing — we won't run into a silenced gat!'

He walked into the joint. Dulcie was holding his arm, and he had two guns in his pocket. He felt kind of weighted down with heaters! Air, warm and acrid with smoke, greeted them.

Johnny slid through the place; went down the passage that led to the apartment. He got to the door; took the weight of his noisy gun in his hand.

The door opened suddenly and Emma Blaine walked right into his arms. He grabbed her with one hand. Her sharp glance was at once fear-filled.

'Gawd! You!'

'Us!' said Johnny, grinning. 'Is Nat in there?'

He watched her expression intently. He didn't expect a useful answer.

'What's going on between you and Nat?' she breathed. 'There's something terrible — I know it — I — '

'I guess you don't know half of it,' snapped Johnny. 'But it's murder, honey! The cops will take in Nat soon. You don't want to be mixed in murder, do you? So talk. Is Billy Death in there?'

'Death!' she croaked. 'Is that his name? Oh, Gawd, let me get out of here!'

'So they're both in there,' breathed Johnny Lebaron. 'Okay, this is where we go to town. Now you walk back in there and leave the doors wide open. What's Nat doin' anyway?'

'He's — he's — packing papers and books out of his safe!'

'Yeah? Must have plenty of phony business. Okay, get in there again. Leave the doors open. Talk to Nat and Billy Death and keep them busy. You wouldn't like to be brought in as an accessory to murder!'

She moaned. Johnny turned her around and opened the door for her. She went in slowly and headed for the other glass door while he waited. He heard the woman talking and knew it wasn't an alert she was handing out. Apparently she intended to look after her skin.

Johnny walked forward with a gun in his right fist. He got a photographic glimpse of Nat Franz, Billy Death and the woman. Then a figure leaped at him from the side of the door, a figure he had not been expecting. It was Ed Kibe, the gunny.

Johnny's gun was knocked down at once. He didn't have time to trigger. Ed Kibe had the advantage of surprise.

Johnny snarled and flexed to throw the man off. He would have done it, but Billy Death and Nat Franz joined the fight. Nat was only half a man because he had only one good hand. Dulcie leaped back and ran. No one went after her because the two-and-a-half men were fully occupied with the enraged Johnny.

Johnny lost his gun. He still had the silenced job in his pocket. He was forced to mill his fists, and so the silenced gun remained where it was. Ed Kibe was playing a hefty part, hanging onto Johnny's shoulders while Billy Death, roused to an unusual anger, tried to grab his fists. Nat Franz slammed a punch into Johnny's guts. The blow hurt but the effort of punching affected Nat's wounded shoulder. He twisted his lips in pain and, while Ed Kibe and Billy Death grappled with the intruder, he picked up a poker from the ornamental fireplace. It was hardly the sort of weapon to brain someone, but Johnny felt it rap him agonisingly on the head. That was the first of a rain of blows. Skin broke and blood trickled.

He jerked his big body in an effort to throw Ed Kibe from his back, wondering why the gunny did not produce a gat and end it in the traditional manner. Then he realised the hood did not want the noise of a gunshot.

Johnny felt blood in his mouth; thought grimly this was the reward of doing the cops' work for free! He hacked at a face before him. The poker struck again and forced a grunt of agony from him. They surged across the room and thudded a chair to the floor. They were like little boys trying to subdue an enraged man-mountain.

Johnny thought this was hell. It flashed on him: where was Dulcie? Anyway, she was well out of this rumpus!

The door closed slowly under the vibrations. The room became an arena filled with the sound of gasping breath and grunts. Feet slithered and thumped against a carpet.

Johnny slammed Billy Death back against a wall with a devastating punch that could have knocked a heavyweight around. The young man came back again, an agonized, determmed look on his face. Psycho or not, he realised the simple fact of the present setup.

The four men milled around. Emma Blaine had gotten out of it. Apparently she had not gone shrieking through the casino for no one came to the room. Johnny was not doing so well now. A number of bangs on the head with a poker doesn't help a man. In addition, Ed Kibe was employing some dirty tactics. He was kicking at Johnny's legs. The kicks cut through to the bone and caused agony.

Two men and a poker, employed grimly, can create havoc with any man. Johnny Lebaron was an ordinary man; no more. He had the ordinary man's guts. He wasn't a gangster. He'd been in the Army and he'd had some tough work as an engineer. He needed all that experience right there in that room. Even so he was going under.

It was the blows with the hard poker that sent him into a daze. Ed Kibe got him slipping, and in a moment Johnny fell to the floor, his face buried in the soft carpet. He gasped for breath and got grit and fluff. He wrenched around, the other men sprawling on top of him like savages.

His struggles were futile when the three men piled on top of him, pinning him down; Nat Franz raised the poker, savagery printed on his face. It was to be a finishing blow.

Johnny rolled his head at the last moment, and the poker hammered the floor. There were curses of 'hold him!' and 'I'll settle him!'

The next moment new sounds crashed

into the room. A door was flung back on its hinges; feet thumped rapidly into the room. Shouts and warning yells swept over Johnny Lebaron. He felt the men leap away from his body.

He got up dazedly. He lurched, blinked through sweat and blood; finally and suddenly got a clear picture of the scene. Cops were in the room. Big, beautiful guys in blue uniforms. At first they filled the room so much that Johnny thought dazedly that there must be a hundred of them; then he realised there were only four. Still, they were four of the most capable cops he had ever seen.

They held on efficiently to Nat Franz, Billy Death and Ed Kibe. The fight sagged from those three men. Ed Kibe suddenly knew he was a sucker. Billy Death was just plain scared. Nat Franz felt the cold dread of future justice.

Then Dulcie was in Johnny's arms, and if she had to hold him up it was the first and only time. 'I got 'em, Johnny! I got 'em! I didn't leave you! I knew I had to get the cops!'

'You're a good gal!'

'Am I?' she smiled twistedly. 'It's the first time you said that, pal, and I love you for it!'

Johnny Lebaron steadied some minutes later. He wiped blood from his face with a handkerchief. His clothes were ruined. Still, he was able to start answering the cops' questions.

'Keep these guys. That one is a hood, probably a killer. The other two are cold-blooded murderers.'

'With a rumpus like this to explain, you wouldn't be kiddin',' grated a cop. 'This dame was yelling about murder. Okay, let's sort it out.'

Johnny talked fast and efficiently and showed the cops the silenced gun. The cops held onto the three scared men. Johnny also took the bull by the horns and told them the story of how he and Dulcie had escaped being murdered at the old water tank in the scrap yard, and how Dulcie, in defending herself, had caused their would-be murderer to fall to his death from the ladder. Dulcie corroborated his version of events, albeit reluctantly.

The incident was news to the cops. The

man's death had never been officially reported. As Johnny had surmised, Nat Franz had arranged to have the body removed and hidden. With her police record, Dulcie was scared that she might yet face some charge concerning the man's death — for manslaughter, if not murder. But before that could happen, the cops would have to find the body and investigate the death scene. Johnny wasn't so worried as Dulcie. He knew the cops would find their fingerprints all over the inside of the tank and along the rim, all of which would help confirm their version of events.

Their stories had to be dished up again when detectives from Headquarters arrived. There was a repeat for the third time when Lieutenant Schwartz, of Homicide, arrived. He was the cop who knew all about the killings of the men Nat Franz had blackmailed and Billy Death had shot. At least, he had known a lot. After ten minutes of listening to Johnny's tale, he knew everything. Judging by the gleam in his eyes, he thought this was quite a great night!

The whole thing was taken down to the police Headquarters and stuck on paper, tidied up, classified and ticketed. The silencer gun was taken to the police laboratory as Exhibit A.

Nat Franz wanted his attorney. The attorney wasn't of much use to him. Nor to Billy Death. The prosecution couldn't link Ed Kibe directly with any killings, but ironically his evidence helped to clear Dulcie completely. On the advice of his attorney, he confessed that, acting on Nat Franz's orders, he had removed the body from the scrapyard and hidden it by burying it in the desert, along with the bloodied rod. He told them where to find it, and the pathologists quickly established that Dulcie's blows to the head and shoulders had not killed him — that had came as the result of a broken neck in his fall from the ladder. And in an attempt to mitigate his sentence Ed Kibe further testified that Nat Franz had told him he had arranged for the dead man to murder Johnny and Dulcie. Nor was that the first such job the man had done — that was why Nat had wanted his death covered up: he didn't want any police investigation into the dead man's activities. That could have led the cops to him. Notwithstanding his co-operation, Ed still finished up with a long stretch in the pen.

The final clincher that cleared both Johnny and Dulcie of any criminal charges was the testimony of Luthor Wade.

* * *

After the trial was finished and Nat Franz and Billy Death awaited the short walk to the chair, Johnny Lebaron decided to go back to New York and Doris. He found it a hard job convincing Dulcie that he was doing the right thing. They spent their last evening together back in their room on Alamo Avenue.

Johnny's plane was due to leave at 10 p.m. and Dulcie was getting worked up. He felt anxious for her but he had to go through with it now.

Dulcie looked up at him appealingly. 'I'm scared, Johnny,' she said huskily.

He held her close. 'There's nothing to

be scared of now, baby, I'll be back. You just see. You just have to trust me.'

'That's right,' she said, 'I've got to. I — I guess I do, Johnny.'

He held her closer. She was warm and passive in his arms; her head rested on his shoulder. It seemed like she wanted to do nothing else but lie there. She was so different to the screeching Dulcie of a few weeks back. He looked down at her hair and could not help but contrast her with the dark-haired Doris who would be waiting for him right now. Gently he pushed her away from him. 'I've got to go, honey,' he said.

She looked up, her blue eyes wide. She held on to his arm as he rose. 'You can't leave me now, Johnny.'

'I've got to. You said you'd trust me.'

She rose swiftly and grabbed him by the shoulders. Her sharp nails bit through the cloth of his jacket.

'I do trust you,' she said. 'I do! But I'm scared. Johnny, I'm scared!'

'I can't stay with you, baby, but I'll try and reach you afterwards like I said I would.'

She gave up suddenly, letting her hands fall. Her eyes were almost tragic. 'Okay, Johnny. I'll stay here. But you'll come back as soon as you can.'

'Yes, I promise.'

He turned away.

She ran in front of him and put her arms around his neck. She lifted up her face and kissed him. She clung to him, trembling. He tried to move her arms, but she wouldn't let go. Finally he pushed them away. With a little sob she turned away from him. At the door he looked back; she was sitting on the divan watching him.

'I'll be back,' he said.

She did not say anything. He closed the door softly behind him. Long after his footsteps had died away she sat upright on the divan, staring at nothing. She was waiting, waiting.

17

The trip to New York gave Johnny Lebaron all the time he needed to come to grips with the problem that was as old as the hills; the brunette versus the blonde. He had a hunch that his reception by his in-laws was going to be red-hot; even so, he figured that Doris was not going to hand him Dulcie on a silver platter. Maybe he should have taken her advice and left his Park Avenue wife on ice.

His hunch was right. Practically the whole family was waiting for him and their hostility charged the air; lay on their refined frozen faces. He saw the hate on Doris's face, he heard it from her lips.

'You've got a nerve! You needn't think you're creeping back here to live in comfort.'

'I want to talk to you, Doris.'

'Get out — go to that ghastly woman — that — '

He wasn't given even the hearing that Nat Franz and his killer had got. He was indicted before he spoke. Maybe they were right. Maybe they were wrong. They didn't want to hear him though.

'You needn't think I was coming back, Doris. If we could only talk quietly together — I've such a lot to explain. You and your family have evidently read the newspapers that wrote up the affair. But it wasn't entirely like that! They had to emphasise the girl — you know how they do it. Look — '

'You must be crazy if you think I'm going to allow you in my house!' hissed her old man.

Johnny walked back to the door. 'Yeah?' he said slowly. 'All I've tried to do is uphold the law. Maybe I did leave Doris, but was I completely to blame? It happens to folks. Okay, have it your own way. You can get a divorce easy enough. Doris, but get a no-fuss one for Hell's sake!'

With that he walked out. It seemed that he had made a complete mess of things, but he still had Dulcie. She'd be waiting for him like she said she would — but would she? Maybe she saw through his promises and even now had given him up to Doris and the life of luxury that went with her. The sooner he got back to Las Vegas the better he'd like it.

He booked a room at an hotel, got the receptionist at the desk to reserve him a ticket at the airport then he turned in for the night.

It was a restless night; a night full of dreams. Nat Franz paid him a visit. Billy Death stood at his side. They pointed accusing fingers at him and he saw himself in the hot chair. Doris was there with her father and all the other fancy panted termites that hitched their wagons to the set up on the Avenue. They were laughing, screaming their aristocratic heads off. He was squirming, he felt the sweat oozing from his body, leaving him weak. The fight was all knocked out of him; until Dulcie showed up with the Governor and a pardon. Then it passed like a cloud, slowly, only to come back, time and again. Then the sun burst forth in all its glory, through the hotel window. He lay there staring at the ceiling, and he felt more contented than he had done for a very long time.

He found himself crooning while he took a shower. Gee, he was on top of the world. He knew now that Dulcie was the only girl for him. Doris could go to Reno and he didn't care how soon.

He was sitting on the edge of the bed smoking when the bellhop came in with a loaded tray and the air ticket to Las Vegas. The coffee smelled good; the food looked good. He realised that he was ravenously hungry. He dropped the weedy looking guy a bill and asked him to call him a taxi in half an hour's time.

He couldn't make that airport quick enough. On the plane he tried to distract his impatience with the line of beauties that stared up at him from the pages of the cheap rag stretched across his lap, but the girls all had something in common; they were all blondes and every one was a Dulcie.

Within two minutes of that plane touching down on the tarmac he was heading in a taxi towards Alamo Avenue. He still had the key to the rooming house and he decided he'd let himself in quietly and creep up on Dulcie from behind. Then after the sob stuff was over they'd paint the town red; that was something he'd never been able to do with Doris.

It was dusk and the neon signs were just making their debut when he finally reached his destination. He looked up at Dulcie's window overlooking the street. The light was on.

His excitement grew now that their reunion was at hand. He went up the steps three at a time. The street door was slightly ajar; not an uncommon thing in a rooming house. He cat-walked through the passage hoping all the time that the old turkey wouldn't show up. His luck was in and he made the first stairs without any interruption from her familiar croak. Outside Dulcie's room he hesitated: he didn't want to scare the life out of her, and he decided to knock. Several minutes passed before the door opened and he could hear his own heartbeats pounding like a hammer in the stillness of that dark, dilapidated landing. Then time stood still as the opening door

revealed a blonde. Was he having night-
mares again? This was no Dulcie. He felt
his guts turn over. He was giddy and the
blood drained from his cheeks as he said,
'I — I seem to have the wrong room.'

The woman was a blonde, but the
blonde wasn't Dulcie.

Johnny turned on his heels and half
stumbled down the stairs. He groped in
the darkness for the landlady's room. He
brought his fist down impatiently on the
door panel, but there was no response.
The old crow was out. In desperation
he retraced his steps back to the landing.
He dragged that crummy looking blonde
back from her rest once again.

She stood on the threshold, hands on
her hips and an amused smirk written all
over her pockmarked face. She made a
feeble attempt at tidying a neglected
hair-do and leaned slightly towards him.

'You're sorta het up, aintcha? What
gives, big boy?'

'Does the name Dulcie Grande mean
anything to you?'

'The dame in the newspapers? Yeah,
she checked outa here a coupla days ago.'

'Did she leave any forwarding address, d'you know?'

The woman eyed him suspiciously like he was a fed or a cop or something. 'If she did, then I wasn't in on it, but I can tell ya one thing: she didn't go of her own accord. That old turkey pitched her out 'cos they just didn't hit it off together.'

Johnny stumbled down the dirty stairs into the street. For once he was out on a limb. The shock had numbed his brain and he stood on the sidewalk trying to sort himself out. The whole thing looked cockeyed; he just couldn't see how she could leave him flat without even a cable or something to let him know what was cooking. He felt like getting soused: a few straight ryes would bring sweet oblivion for a few hours. Pulling down the brim of his hat he took a last look up at Duicie's window and beat it in the direction of the nearest Nightery.

There was a steady drizzle of rain and the flashing neons were mirrored in the puddles as he walked blindly on, his big fists thrust deep into the pockets of his jacket.

The sidewalks were busy with homeward bound workers from the city. They bore down on him like an army intent on blocking his path; with head well down he sidetracked them one by one as their hurrying feet approached the circle of his limited vision. Dulcie might have been in that throng but he wouldn't have seen her; he was too doggone depressed to see anything.

Oblivious to the discomfort of hunger, cold and the saturation of the ever-increasing rain driven by a fierce wind, he walked blindly on. He began to curse under his breath. Women sure spelled trouble to a guy; maybe he'd been a sucker all along with them. Maybe he should have had his fill then moved on to the next: one night stands. Blondes, brunettes and redheads, treat them all the same so long as they had what a guy needed most.

He forgot his objective, which was a straight rye, and continued to walk until his footsteps began to echo through the silent streets.

Dulcie Grande had a hunch that Johnny would show up at the airport in spite of the reply cablegram from Doris that now lay creased up in the bottom of her handbag. She would've bet a million dollars to a dime that Johnny hadn't a clue to her change of address. If he'd decided to stay in New York for keeps he would have wired her himself, not left it to that diamond crusted wife of his to do his dirty work for him.

In spite of the showdown she'd had with the old turkey at the rooming house, she'd persuaded her to give Johnny a message if he showed up. She wondered what he was doing right now and how he'd squared up to that high faluting family of Doris's. They'd have put him on ice for sure over the front page stuff the *Tribune* had scooped.

She'd gotten herself a new address overlooking the park. Since Johnny had been gone, time had almost stood still.

She'd sat on a bench under the trees and scanned the society columns of the morning papers, hoping to read that Doris was going to Reno. The change in her routine had brought back a healthy pink glow to her cheeks and she felt like a reincarnation of the old Dulcie; just the way Johnny would have liked her.

She decided to drive over to the airport. By the time she'd got her car out of the parking lot, it was dusk and a cold rain had settled in for the night. Reaching her destination she made a beeline for the reception hall and studied the passenger lists. She ran her finger down the column of names; Oscar Goldberg; Rachael Goldberg; James L. Bentwick; and then her heart missed a beat — Johnny!

She forgot the way the guy at the information desk had tried to get fresh with her the day before; instead, she felt like kissing him all the while she showered him with questions.

He looked at his watch. 'The Clipper your boyfriend was on wasn't due in here until 7.10 — but that plane was ahead of schedule by 30 minutes. If he's not around then you've missed him.'

She hurried out on to the tarmac.

He watched her go and called out to her, 'Too bad, baby.'

There wasn't a sign of Johnny but she wasn't grieving because it was only a matter of time before he caught up with her. She raced her auto with all it had got back to Alamo Avenue. If Johnny still wanted her, that would be where he was heading. She pulled up outside the rooming house with a screeching of brakes. The front door was open and she hurried up the stairs to her old room. The crummy blonde, her successor to the tenancy, was coming down the last flight. She looked like she was going to hit the high spots by the way she was rigged up. She was the first to speak. 'He's been here looking for you. He's a real nice guy and — '

Dulcie cut her short. 'Where'd he go? You must help me.'

The woman slid a motherly hand on Dulcie's sleeve. 'You got it bad, huh?'

Dulcie was impatient with the woman. 'What did he say? Where did he go? D'you know if he got my note down-stairs?'

'He didn't get no note. The old turkey's been out all day. I couldn't tell him nothing. I didn't know about the note, He just went, and he looked all washed up.'

Dulcie slipped her the price of a bottle of rye, and got back in her auto. She looked down the sidewalk and wondered how far Johnny had gone. She toured the city all evening. Every nightery, every dive, every poolroom — but no Johnny.

It was 2 a.m. when she finally returned to her apartment. Next morning she was up early. The day was bright and she stood looking out of the window across to the park. The trees and the flowerbeds had a freshness about them that only the rain can bring. She wondered if any breaks would come her way today.

Then she saw him. At first she put it down to hallucinations. He was asleep on a bench in the park not so very far from her window. Her Johnny! She knew then that he was the only guy for her.

Bedroom doors opened in succession and a dozen pairs of sleepy eyes watched her mad dash down the stairs, and blindly across the road. The man driving a yellow cab let loose a torrent of nasty words, like only hackies can, as he missed her, inches only short of his fender.

Johnny was half up out of his seat and she almost fell into his arms. 'Johnny — oh, Johnny!' she cried.

'Dulcie,' he said and drew her closer.

The hackie looked back, and grinned.

THE END

We do hope that you have enjoyed reading this large print book.

Did you know that all of our titles are available for purchase?

We publish a wide range of high quality large print books including:
Romances, Mysteries, Classics
General Fiction
Non Fiction and Westerns

Special interest titles available in large print are:
The Little Oxford Dictionary
Music Book, Song Book
Hymn Book, Service Book

Also available from us courtesy of Oxford University Press:
Young Readers' Dictionary
(large print edition)
Young Readers' Thesaurus
(large print edition)

For further information or a free brochure, please contact us at:
Ulverscroft Large Print Books Ltd.,
The Green, Bradgate Road, Anstey,
Leicester, LE7 7FU, England.
Tel: (00 44) **0116 236 4325**
Fax: (00 44) **0116 234 0205**